Katie's swift intake of breath sounded unnaturally loud. 'It is very warm in here...' She gazed about in a pathetic attempt to distract him.

Rigo's low voice pulsed with intent. 'I don't think it's that sort of heat I can feel. Well, *signorina*?' he pressed. 'There must be something other than my swimming technique that kept you fascinated...'

Mutely, she shook her head. It was blood heat in the leisure suite, and almost dark. Just the pool lights shimmering behind her like dots of moonlight on a lake. She felt cornered by a powerful predator—a predator she had sought out—and now her reward was to be wrapped in a cloak of arousal as she waited to see what would happen next.

Susan Stephens was a professional singer before meeting her husband on the tiny Mediterranean island of Malta. In true Modern™ Romance style they met on Monday, became engaged on Friday and were married three months after that. Almost thirty years and three children later, they are still in love. (Susan does not advise her children to return home one day with a similar story, as she may not take the news with the same fortitude as her own mother!)

Susan had written several non-fiction books when fate took a hand. At a charity costume ball there was an after-dinner auction. One of the lots, 'Spend a Day with an Author', had been donated by Mills & Boon® author Penny Jordan. Susan's husband bought this lot, and Penny was to become not just a great friend but a wonderful mentor, who encouraged Susan to write romance.

Susan loves her family, her pets, her friends and her writing. She enjoys entertaining, travel, and going to the theatre. She reads, cooks, and plays the piano to relax, and can occasionally be found throwing herself off mountains on a pair of skis or galloping through the countryside. Visit Susan's website: www.susanstephens.net—she loves to hear from her readers all around the world!

Recent books by the same author:

Modern™ Romance
COUNT MAXIME'S VIRGIN
DESERT KING, PREGNANT MISTRESS
BOUGHT: ONE ISLAND, ONE BRIDE

The Royal House of Niroli
EXPECTING HIS ROYAL BABY—*Book 5*

Modern Heat™
HOUSEKEEPER AT HIS BECK AND CALL

ITALIAN BOSS, PROUD MISS PRIM

BY
SUSAN STEPHENS

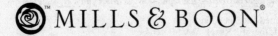

All the characters in this book have no existence outside the imagination of the author, and have no relation whatsoever to anyone bearing the same name or names. They are not even distantly inspired by any individual known or unknown to the author, and all the incidents are pure invention.

First published in Great Britain 2009
Harlequin Mills & Boon Limited,
Eton House, 18-24 Paradise Road, Richmond, Surrey TW9 1SR

© Susan Stephens 2009

ISBN: 978 0 263 87440 2

Set in Times Roman 10½ on 12 pt
01-1009-49554

Harlequin Mills & Boon policy is to use papers that are natural, renewable and recyclable products and made from wood grown in sustainable forests. The logging and manufacturing process conform to the legal environmental regulations of the country of origin.

Printed and bound in Spain
by Litografia Rosés, S.A., Barcelona

ITALIAN BOSS, PROUD MISS PRIM

For Jenny, who is both inspired and inspiring.

CHAPTER ONE

SIX hours, fifteen minutes in the same hard chair at the same desk, in the same cold office, in the same northern town...

She'd lost the will to live.

Almost...

Arranging a telephone conference with Signor Rigo Ruggiero in Rome was a pain, even for a young lawyer as tenacious as Katie Bannister, because first she had to get past Ruggiero's army of snooty retainers.

Let me speak to him in person, screeched inner Katie, whilst outwardly Katie was calm. Well, she had to be—she was a respected professional.

With no inner life at all.

No inner life? Hmm, wouldn't that make things easy? Unfortunately, Katie was blessed with a vivid imagination and an active fantasy life, and it was always getting her into trouble. Dumpy, plain and unprepossessing became sharp and confident in the blink of an eye—especially over the phone.

In her junior position at the small solicitor's firm, Katie wouldn't normally be expected to deal with such a high-profile client, but this was a trivial matter, according to the senior partner, and if she wanted to work her way up the profession it would be good for Katie to cut her teeth on—

'*Pronto…*'

At last. *At last!* 'Signor Ruggiero?'

'*Sì…?*'

The deep-pitched voice speared a shiver down her spine. But gut instinct wasn't enough. Did it prove the identity of the speaker? Spoken Italian was sexy; distractingly so. Quickly gathering her thoughts, Katie picked up her notes and went through the security checks she had drawn up.

To his credit, Signor Ruggiero answered them all accurately and politely. To her dismay her imagination insisted on working overtime as she nursed the phone—tall, dark and handsome didn't begin to cover it. Still, this was going better than she had expected after her run-in with his staff. Now it was simply a matter of informing the Italian tycoon that he was the chief beneficiary in his late brother's will.

'My late *step*brother's will,' he corrected her.

The honey-rich baritone had acquired an edge of steel. He sounded stern, cold, uninterested.

A man who was so hard to contact would hardly want chit-chat, Katie reminded herself, moving up a gear. 'My apologies, Signor Ruggiero, your late *step*brother's will…'

As the conversation continued Katie picked up more clues. If there was one thing she was good at it was reading people's voices. Time spent training to be an opera singer at one of the world's foremost music conservatoires had allowed her well-tuned ear to instantly evaluate a voice, and this one had both practised charm and a killer edge.

'Can we cut to the chase, Signorina Bannister?'

And cut out print yards of legalese? 'Certainly…'

Katie's reputation at the firm was founded on dogged persistence along with her ability to calm even the most fractious of clients, but after a long day in a cheap suit in a cold office, she was at the end of her tether. It wasn't as if she was trying to serve a writ, for goodness' sake; rather she was trying to inform Signor Ruggiero that he had come into money.

More money, Katie qualified, glancing at the magazine the girls in the office had so helpfully placed on her desk. It featured a devastatingly handsome Rigo Ruggiero on the front cover. Not that she was interested. Firming her jaw, she continued to explain to one of the richest men in Italy why she must come to see him in person. To Rome, where she had thought of going as a singer, once…

'Well, I haven't got the time to come over there—'

Katie snapped back to the present. 'Your stepbrother anticipated this…' Her heart picked up pace as she went on to read out the letter of instruction that came with the will. She was normally unflappable, but office tittle-tattle had unsettled her where Rigo Ruggiero was concerned. He was not just a successful tycoon, but a high-profile playboy who lived life in the fast lane. To say that Katie Bannister and Rigo Ruggiero were worlds apart was a massive understatement.

Everyone in the office had thought it highly amusing that the official office virgin had been appointed to deal with Italy's most notorious playboy. Katie's public face had remained unmoved through all this teasing banter, but her imagination had run riot. After her initial trepidation, she had thought, bring it on. What did she have to worry about? Rigo Ruggiero would take one look at dull little Katie Bannister and she'd be safe.

'No, I'm sorry,' she said. 'I'm afraid your late stepbrother's personal effects cannot be sent to you through the post, Signor Ruggiero.'

'Why not?'

'Because…' She took a deep, steadying breath. Forget the letter of intentions—shouldn't he care a little more? And did he have to snap like that? His stepbrother had just died, for goodness' sake. Surely he was curious to learn what he'd been left in the will? 'Your stepbrother's instructions are *most* specific, Signor Ruggiero. He appointed the firm I represent, Flintock, Gough and Coverdale, as executors to his will, and Mr Flintock has asked me to carry out the requirements therein to the letter—'

'Therein?'

Mockery now?

'Do you always speak legalese to your clients, Signorina Bannister? That must be very confusing for them.' His voice was dry and amused. 'I recommend plain-speaking myself…'

No one had ever criticised her dedication to the letter of the law before and it was becoming increasingly clear that Rigo Ruggiero couldn't care a fig for his stepbrother. She could see him now, lolling back on some easy chair as he took the call—all preposterously white teeth, inky black hair and dark, mocking eyes. Closing her eyes, she willed herself to remain calm. 'What I'm trying to explain, Signor Ruggiero—'

'Don't patronise me.'

The tone of voice both stung and acted as a warning. 'I apologise. That was not my intention.'

'Then I forgive you…'

In a voice like a caress. Was he flirting with her? Unlikely as that seemed, it appeared so, and her body definitely agreed. 'So could we fix an appointment?' she suggested, returning determinedly to the point of the call.

There was silence at the other end of the line, but somehow worldly amusement managed to travel down it anyway. 'Whenever you like,' he murmured.

The throaty drawl was enough to make her body quiver with anticipation. Katie stared out of the window at the cold, autumnal Yorkshire rain. That was the swiftest return to reality she could imagine. Beneath her conventional, even plain exterior, lurked a seam of wanderlust. She had dreamed at one time that it would be the opera houses of the world she'd be visiting. Did she have the courage to make this trip to Rome in her new guise as solicitor, or would the loss of her singing voice be a reminder that was too painful to bear?

'Well,' the deep male voice demanded, 'I don't have all day, Signorina Bannister. When would you like to meet?'

She longed for a break, and she could be in Rome tomorrow. Before she could stop herself the words tumbled out. 'What about tomorrow, Signor Ruggiero? If that's convenient for you…?'

'I'll make it so,' he said.

'Thank you for your cooperation.' She could hardly breathe her heart was thundering so fast. Talking over the phone was easy, but when Signor Ruggiero saw how plain and boring she was in person… And when she saw Rome…

'I look forward to meeting you,' he said. 'You have a lovely voice, by the way.'

A lovely voice… 'Thank you…' Playboys were expected to flirt, and Signor Ruggiero couldn't be expected to know that her voice had been reduced to husky ashes after a fire in her student lodgings. She had been overjoyed in the hospital when she found out all her friends had escaped uninjured, and devastated to discover that after inhaling too much smoke her voice had been reduced for good to a croak. Oddly enough, people who didn't know her history found that husky sound attractive. But that wasn't her only legacy from the fire. She would never sing again and had enough scars on her back to ensure no one would ever see her naked. When her singing career had crashed to a close, she had set about forging a new life as a lawyer. This was a life in the shadows rather than the spotlight, but she wasn't interested in the spotlight; it was the music she missed.

'Signorina Bannister? Are you still there?'

'I beg your pardon, Signor Ruggiero. I just knocked something off my desk.'

Or wished she had, Katie thought, staring at the magazine. A towering powerhouse of hard, tanned muscle, dressed in a sharp designer suit, stared back at her from the front cover. Rigo Ruggiero couldn't even be accused of having a smooth, rich boy's face. His verged on piratical, complete with sharp black stubble and a dangerous gleam in night-dark, emerald eyes. Add to that a shock of thick black hair and a jaw even firmer than her own—

'You haven't changed your mind about our meeting, I hope?'

There was a faint edge of challenge to his voice that her body responded to with enthusiasm. 'Not at all,' she reassured him firmly. Reaching across the desk, she was about to send the magazine flying to the floor when she paused. The cynical curve of his mouth set her teeth on edge, but she had to admit it was the perfect frame for his arrogant voice. And, as if there wasn't enough perfection in his life, the image showed him with his arm draped around the shoulders of a blonde girl so achingly lovely she looked like a doll rather than a living, breathing woman.

It would be fine, Katie told herself, straightening up. She could do this. The trip to Rome was business and no one could distract her from that.

'I have a question for you, Signorina Bannister.'

'Yes?' Tightening her grip on the phone, Katie realised she was still transfixed by the image of the girl's unblemished skin.

'Why you?' he rapped.

This was no playboy, but a merciless tycoon questioning the wisdom of sending such a young and inexperienced lawyer to meet with him. But he had a point. Why were they sending her? Because she spoke fluent Italian, thanks to her opera training, Katie reasoned, because she was plain, safe and unattached, and, as the newest recruit to the firm, she had little or no say when it came to apportioning work.

Better not let on she was so junior. 'I'm the only solicitor in the firm who could spare the time to come to Rome—'

'You're not much good, then?'

'Signor Ruggiero—'

'Piano, piano, bella...'

Piano, bella? He was telling her to calm down—and in a voice he might use with a lover.

Italian was sexy, Katie reminded herself. The language itself had a lyrical music all its own. And when you added Rigo Ruggiero to the mix—

'So,' he said, 'I'll see you in Rome tomorrow—*sì?*'

See him tomorrow...

He was quicksilver to her caution, one moment stern, the next amused. But he was right to be suspicious about her credentials. She wasn't a great lawyer. She never would be a great lawyer because she didn't have the hunger for it. She sometimes wondered if the passion she'd felt for her operatic career would ever transfer to anything else. But the firm she had worked for since she had retrained as a solicitor had been good to her when her life had gone up in flames, and now she was scarred a role in the background suited her.

'I'll expect you tomorrow.'

Tomorrow...

This was exactly what she'd asked for. But since she'd suggested tomorrow her confidence had been slowly seeping away. The whole idea was ridiculous. How could she go to Rome, the city where she had dreamed of being part of the musical life, only as a second-rate lawyer to deal with one of the most acute minds around?

The only reason Katie could think of was hard, economic reality. The senior partner at her firm was talking redundancies, thanks to the economic downturn, and as last into the firm she was most likely to be first out. There was no question this trip to Rome and her meeting with someone as high-profile as Rigo Ruggiero would add some much-needed colour to her CV.

It made sense—well, to everything except her self-confidence. How could Katie Bannister, dressed by the cheapest store in town, the girl who wouldn't know a fashion must-have if she fell over it, meet with the world's most notorious playboy and come out of that meeting unscathed?

The plain and simple truth was, she had to.

'I'll book a flight,' she said, thinking out loud.

'I'd recommend it,' the man in question interrupted dryly. 'Mail me with the details and I'll make sure someone is at Fiumicino Airport to meet you—'

'That's very—'

Katie stared at the dead receiver in her hands. How rude. Or look at it another way, she persuaded herself; this was a challenge, and she was hardly a stranger to that.

She had laughed when the other girls at the firm had insisted that Katie Bannister had hidden fire and would master the maverick playboy in less time than it took to say hold my briefs—maybe she had possessed that fire once, but not now—and the girls in the office hadn't spoken to him, a man so cold and heartless he could discuss a close relative's bequest without so much as a play of regret. And end a conversation without any of the usual niceties. Rigo Ruggiero was clearly an indulged and arrogant monster and the sooner her business with him was concluded the better she would like it.

It was just a shame her body disagreed.

She'd cope with that too. Palming her mouse, Katie brought up flight schedules to Rome. Could she make it there and back in one day? She would try her very best to do so.

Having replaced the receiver in its nest, Rigo settled back in his leather swivel chair. In spite of the unwelcome message Katie Bannister had delivered from a man he'd hoped never to hear from again, the young lawyer had made him smile.

Because he liked her voice?

It had certainly scored highly in several categories: it was female; it was young; it was husky; it was sexy. Very sexy. And intelligent. And…sexy. He already had an image of her in his mind.

So, he reflected, returning to the purpose of Signorina Bannister's call, his stepbrother had left him something in his will. A poisoned chalice? Shares in a crime syndicate? What? He stood up and started pacing. Why should the man who had shown him nothing but contempt and hatred since the day he had walked into his life leave him anything at all in his will? And what was it about these personal effects that made them so precious only a representative from a solicitor's firm in England could hand-deliver them?

He knew Carlo had been living in the north of England for some years, thanks to the headlines in the papers detailing his stepbrother's countless misdemeanours, and could confidently predict that if these personal effects were gold bars they'd be stolen—likewise jewellery, antiques or art. What else would Carlo care enough about not to chance it going astray? It had to be something incriminating—something that gave Carlo one last stab at him before the gates of hell closed on his stepbrother for ever.

Rigo had been just fourteen when his father married again

and seventeen when he had left home for good. He had left home after a couple of years of Carlo's vicious tricks, when home became a cruel misnomer for somewhere Rigo was no longer welcome. How he had longed for his father's love, but that love had found another home. So he conquered his regret and left the countryside to pursue his dreams in Rome. He hadn't heard from Carlo, his elder by eleven years, from that day to this.

But he had a lot to thank Carlo for, Rigo reflected, standing by the floor-to-ceiling windows in his luxurious penthouse overlooking Rome. He lived in the most exclusive part of the city and this was only one of his many properties. Leaving the country all those years ago had led to success, wealth and, more important in his eyes, the chance to live life the way he believed it should be led.

These thoughts brought him back full circle to the girl from England he must somehow fit into his busy schedule tomorrow. Crossing to his desk, he scanned his diary. He'd just sacked the latest in a long line of hopeless PAs. Finding a reliable replacement was proving harder than he had anticipated.

Which left a vacancy on his staff…

If she was half as intriguing as her husky voice suggested, he would gladly clear his diary for Signorina Bannister. He would make the whole of tomorrow free just for her.

CHAPTER TWO

KATIE was having second thoughts. Just packing a few essentials for the trip in her shabby bag proved she wasn't the right person for this job. She might have the heart to handle Rigo Ruggiero, but she lacked the panache. The firm should be sending someone sharp and polished to Rome, someone sophisticated, who spoke the same sophisticated language as him. Two new packets of tights and a clean white blouse did not a sophisticate make, but it was the best she could do. There was nothing in her wardrobe suitable for spending time in Rome with a man renowned for his sartorial elegance.

A few calming breaths later Katie had worked out that, as she couldn't compete, she shouldn't try. She should look at what she was—a competent young lawyer from a small firm in the north of England, which meant a brown suit and low-heeled brown court shoes were the perfect choice.

This wasn't a holiday, Katie reminded herself sternly, though as an afterthought she added a pair of comfortable trousers and a sweater. With the tight schedule she had planned it was unlikely there would be any off-duty time, but if there was she could dress for that too.

But everything was brown, even her bag, Katie noticed as she prepared to close the door on her small terraced house. A life in the shadows was one thing, but she hadn't noticed the colour seeping from it. Perhaps it had gone with the music…

She shook herself round determinedly. She was going to Rome—not as a singer as she had always hoped, but as a representative of a respectable legal firm. How many people got a second chance like that?

Locking the door, she tested the handle and picked up her bag. Tipping her chin at a confident angle, she walked briskly down the path. She was going to Italy to meet one of the most exciting men of his day. She didn't expect to be part of Rigo Ruggiero's life but, for a few short and hopefully thrilling hours, she would be an observer. At the very least she could report back to the girls in the office and brighten up their coffee breaks for the foreseeable future.

Signor Ruggiero had lied. Clutching her sensible bag like a comfort blanket, Katie stood bewildered amongst the crowds on the pavement outside Fiumicino Airport in Rome. The sun was beating down like an unrelenting spotlight and the heat was overpowering. She stared this way and that, but it only confirmed what she already knew, which was, no one had come to meet her. Plus everyone else seemed to know where they were going. She was the only country bumpkin who appeared to be cast adrift in the big city.

And was fervently wishing she'd handled her own transport arrangements into Rome.

What was wrong with her? She had the address…

Having found it in her bag, she looked for a taxi. Was she going to be defeated before she even started this adventure? But each time she stepped forward to claim an empty cab, someone taller, slicker and more confident than Katie stepped in front of her—

'Signorina Bannister?'

The voice reached into her chest and squeezed her heart tight before she even had chance to look around, and when she did she almost stumbled into the arms of a man who put his photographs to shame. Her heart drummed an immediate tattoo. Rigo Ruggiero in the hard, tanned flesh was infinitely better-looking than his air-brushed images—so hot you wouldn't touch him without protective clothing. He was the type of man Katie had spent her whole life dreaming about and wishing would notice her, but who, of course, never would—other than today, when he had no alternative.

'Sorry…sorry.' She righted herself quickly before he was brought into contact with her cheap polyester suit. 'Signorina Bannister? That's me.'

'Are you sure?'

Her cheeks flamed. 'Of course I'm sure…'

Thrusting her serviceable bag beneath her arm, she held out her free hand in greeting. 'This is very good of you, sir—' She braced herself for contact.

Contact there was none.

Startlingly green and uncomfortably shrewd eyes refused to share Signor Ruggiero's practised smile. He was not the man in the magazine photograph. That man was a playboy with pleasure on his mind. The man in front of her was a realist, a thinker, a business tycoon, and he took no prisoners. The hand she had extended dropped back to her side. 'I didn't think you would come to meet me in person—'

'It is my pleasure to do so.'

He even bowed slightly, but his tone suggested it was anything but a pleasure for him.

Katie's worst fears were confirmed. Rigo Ruggiero was hiding disappointment. Having heard her husky voice over the phone, he had imagined he had come to the airport to meet a siren. They had both been misled, Katie reflected wryly. Now this was not business for her; it had become personal. Rigo Ruggiero had shadows behind his eyes she couldn't resist and wanted to understand, and he was so handsome he made her heart ache.

'You had a good journey, I hope.'

'Very good, thank you.' She registered the fact that he had spoken to her in a tone of voice she imagined he might use with a maiden aunt. He was so much taller, bigger and had a more powerful aura than her imagination had allowed and was far more rugged. He was the type of man who could look dangerous even in tailored clothes. The dark trousers complemented his athletic figure and the crisp blue shirt was open a couple of buttons at the neck, revealing a hard, tanned chest, shaded with black hair. The sight of this gave parts of her that were largely unused a vigorous workout. If this wasn't lust at first sight, it was the closest Katie Bannister had ever come to it.

But what she needed now, Katie reasoned with her sensible head on, was some form of identification to prove to Rigo Ruggiero she was who she said she was. On plundering her bag she managed to spill the contents all over his designer-clad feet.

'Allow me, Signorina Bannister…'

To his credit, he immediately dipped to rescue her passport, tickets, toffees, tissues and all the other embarrassing detritus she had accumulated during the flight.

'Why don't I take your bag?' he suggested, staring her straight in the eyes as he straightened up.

My shabby, disreputable-looking bag? 'That's very kind of you. And here's my passport for purposes of identification.'

'I don't think we'll need that,' he said, lips pressing down in an unfeasibly attractive way. And then, in a final cataclysmic put-down, he suggested, 'Why don't you put your passport somewhere safe before you lose it?'

So she wasn't a maiden aunt, she was a child.

She'd made a great first impression. He even held the bag steady for her as she stuffed her possessions back inside. She glanced at him apologetically. He had no need to flag it up. Her clothes, her gaucheness, her red cheeks and clumsiness, all told a story Rigo Ruggiero had no interest in reading.

'And my stepbrother's personal effects?' he pressed, gazing past her.

She wondered if he expected a packing case to be following on. 'Your stepbrother's effects are right here.' She patted the breast pocket of her jacket to reassure him.

'That doesn't look like very much.'

'Well, it is a very small package.' She blushed violently to see him conceal a smile.

'OK,' he said, neither agreeing nor disagreeing, 'I'll get the car.'

'Honestly, I'm quite happy to take a cab—'

'So we arrive at my penthouse in convoy?' he suggested, shooting her a look.

How much better could this get? 'See your point,' she murmured with a nervous laugh.

How much better? A lot better, Katie realised as a blood-red sports car drew up at the kerb. She didn't need to remember the blonde in the magazine to know she was hardly in this class. A sick, heavy feeling was building in her stomach as an admiring crowd gathered around the high-performance vehicle and its elegant driver. They had recognised Rigo, of course, and now they were eager to find out who he was meeting at the airport.

That was what she had to walk through to get to the car.

'I don't bite, Signorina Bannister.'

The throaty drawl drew her attention to the man leaning over the roof of the low-slung sex-machine.

A laugh rippled through the crowd as she locked gazes

with him. Everyone was staring at her and she could feel their disappointment. She was not some famous beauty or a super-model. She was about the furthest thing from that you could get. Steeling herself, she took the half-dozen steps required to close the distance between herself and the car. Signor Ruggiero had already stowed her bag, and so all she had to do was get in—but that meant she had to slot herself into an impossibly narrow-looking opening.

'When you're ready,' he drawled.

She had already anticipated that folding her inelegant body into such an elegant car was a skill she didn't possess. She was right and, to her horror, she got stuck.

What made it worse was that Signor Ruggiero came to help her, and all but lifted her into the formed seat, which she now discovered had been moulded around a fairy's bottom.

But at least she was out of sight of the crowd, Katie reasoned as he slid into the driver's seat beside her.

'Comfortable?' He glanced at her to check.

'Perfectly.' On edge.

Now she had to convince herself that you couldn't die from the shock of meeting a man like this in person, and that the air in the confined cabin hadn't changed with an overload of ions and his delicious scent. But it had. And it was charged with something else…sex, Katie realised, primly tugging down her skirt. Rigo Ruggiero radiated sex.

'You can understand my impatience, I'm sure,' he said.

She gripped the seat as the engine roared like a jet.

'This bequest from such an unexpected quarter has in-trigued me,' he went on.

This was business, she told herself in a silent shout, but that reassurance was growing a little thin.

'I ask myself,' he said, 'what can be so important that only a personal delivery of the documents would do?'

As he glanced at her, Katie thought: And by a girl like this? She shrank beneath a gaze that took in every stitch of man-made fibre until finally it came to rest on her sensible, low-heeled shoes. She quickly tucked her feet away, out of sight.

'I'm sorry if I kept you waiting.'

He shrugged. 'I must have missed you, somehow.'

Searching for that husky-voiced siren would do it every time.

'But never mind,' he added dryly, flashing that wolf smile of his. 'I've got you now.'

'Indeed you do.'

He shrugged as he released the brake and pulled away. The adventure begins, Katie thought, hoping she was up to it. She didn't need Signor Ruggiero to spell it out. Katie Bannister was hardly the type of woman he would normally put himself out for.

She held on tightly to the seat as he steered smoothly away from the kerb. 'Ten kilometres an hour OK for you?' he murmured as they joined a crawling stream of traffic.

'Sorry, I'm just not used to…'

How many people were used to driving in a sports car? Katie asked herself sensibly. She had entered a world that was completely alien to her, and it would take a while to adjust. Closing her eyes and wishing herself a million miles away wouldn't work this time, because this time she really was living the fantasy.

She didn't realise how tense she had become until she heard Signor Ruggiero say, 'Don't worry, Signorina Bannister. I shall strive to achieve a balance between my impatience and your obvious lack of confidence in my driving ability—'

'Oh, I'm not—' Her mouth slammed shut when she realised too late he was mocking her. And now the set of his jaw did nothing to encourage conversation.

He was hardly her typical client, but this sort of impatience was universal. The reading of a will was notoriously full of surprises and, whether those surprises turned out to be bad or good, human nature demanded answers fast.

Katie's hand crept to the breast pocket of her suit, where she wished fervently for some last small legacy of love for him contained within the envelope she was carrying—though, if past experience was any guide, she was wasting her time.

OK, so meeting Katie Bannister had been a shock, but he was growing used to her unique vibe. She was as different from the women he was used to mixing with as it was possible to imagine, but that wasn't necessarily a bad thing, only different. He didn't need false breasts and false smiles—but neither did he need complications. Signorina Bannister was a quiet little mouse and awkward, which meant he would have to spend more time with her than he had anticipated, but how could he throw her to the wolves in Rome? She was out of her comfort zone and had anticipated more time to prepare before meeting him. She found herself in a much bigger, faster world than her comfortable country cocoon and would have to adapt quickly. Meanwhile they had a forty-five minute journey ahead of them and he couldn't stand this uncomfortable silence. 'I'd like you to call me Rigo.'

She bit her lip. Her pale cheeks blazed. She said precisely nothing.

Ducking his head, he checked the road before steering north-east to Rome. It gave him an excuse to flash a glance at her. 'Try it,' he said, thinking she looked like a rabbit trapped in headlights. 'Rrr…igo…'

She pressed back in her seat. He felt instinctively that this was someone to whom life had not always been kind. Did he have time to be a social worker? OK, so she brought out his protective instinct, but he was no bleeding heart. Perhaps it would help if he let her know he was no threat to her—absolutely no threat at all. 'You don't even have to say my name in Italian,' he said dryly. 'English will do.'

She said his name—a little reluctantly, he thought. *'Bene,'* he said. 'That was very good.'

'And you can call me Signorina Bannister,' she said.

He laughed. And for the first time that day, he relaxed. 'Very well, Signorina Bannister,' he agreed. 'Your wish is my command…' At least on the subject of names.

CHAPTER THREE

MAYBE the client was always right, but she was going to keep this formal. She would never get used to a man like Rigo Ruggiero in the short time available as he seemed to think she could, and so it was better not to try.

But that didn't mean she couldn't enjoy this quietly. This tasty slice of *la dolce vita* was her first real adventure. Rigo Ruggiero—Roma, Italia—a real-life Italian playboy driving a blood-red sports car with Katie Bannister sitting next to him. The closest she had ever come to this before was in her fantasy world.

The view from the tinted window was extraordinary. They had cleared the boring industrial places and were driving into Rome. It was like entering the pages of a living history book—if one with a serious traffic problem, traffic Rigo Ruggiero had no problem negotiating. Her confidence had grown, Katie realised, noting how relaxed she had become. She could get used to this—the Colosseum here…Trajan's Market there. The only place she dared not look was to her left, in case Signor Ruggiero thought she was staring at him. But she didn't need to stare to know he wa built like a gladiator and had the commanding face of a Roman general. She could feel that in every part of her.

'Trajan's Market has recently been reopened to the public.'

She refocused as he spoke. This conversational tone was not what she expected from the gladiator in her head, but then she hadn't expected him to speak at all. Signor Ruggiero was being kind by entering into conversation with her—and at least it gave her an excuse to stare at him. 'Really?'

She knew her eager gaze was gauche, but he was perfection, which made it hard not to stare. If she could have designed a man, this would be him. Even her imagination couldn't have mapped a face so perfect or a body made for uninterrupted sin—

'Even in AD 113,' he went on, 'these large shopping malls were in demand.'

As he smiled, a flash of strong white teeth against his tan made her think even more wicked thoughts. She could think of a better use for those firm, mobile lips and those wolf teeth, and when he angled that rough, stubble-shaded chin towards the remarkably well-preserved Roman buildings she felt a pulse begin to throb where it had absolutely no business doing so. Did he know the effect he was having on her? Katie wondered, blushing when he looked at her for her opinion. Hopefully not.

'I read somewhere that Trajan's Market was the experiment in bringing shops together under one roof,' she said, trying to seem gripped by Roman history when the only thing she wanted to be gripped by was him.

His face creased in an attractive smile. 'It was the first—unless you know of one dating from earlier times, of course?'

She shook her head. Obviously he knew more than she did about his own city, but she remained silent, because she thought it was safer to keep things formal rather than to chat. And she had only visited one shopping mall in her whole life. The girls from the office had persuaded her to accompany them and she had vowed, never again! The lights, the crowds jostling her, the shops full of things she didn't need or want. Give her the wide open spaces in the country any day…

'I think Rome is going to be quite an eye-opener for you.'

You could say that again, Katie thought as Rigo steered the sports car down a fashionable shopping street with more glitz and glamour than her poor fantasies could hope to conjure up.

Katie's head was still spinning with all the lavish things she'd seen when she sat down in Rigo's vast, ultra-modern study. Light flooded in, revealing every flaw—or would have done had there been any, but, as she might have imagined, Rigo lived in unimaginable luxury. His penthouse was immaculate, and his study boasted every conceivable high-tech man-toy. She found it starkly beautiful, with its colour scheme of steel and white. There was glass everywhere and vibrant modern art on the walls. Incredibly, the roof could be open to the sky, which it was. Her jaw dropped as she stared up to watch birds wheeling overhead in a flawless cobalt sky. So this was how the rich lived. After the chaos and bustle of the city streets, Rigo's eyrie at the very top of an ancient *palazzo* was a haven of quiet. She could even hear the birds singing if she held her breath.

Katie forced her attention away from the aerial display as Rigo came to sit across the desk from her. He sprawled in such a relaxed fashion, while she was anxiously perching on the very edge of one of his divine cream leather chairs. It was showroom-new, like the huge glass desk in front of her—and that was another concern. What if she left a smudge on its pristine surface?

'Do you like the view?' he prompted.

'I love it.' There were windows to three sides overlooking the rooftops of Rome, but Rigo's husky baritone attracted her more. Her heart squeezed tight as he looked out of the window and she looked at him. He was so perfect. And she would never know him, not properly. But she would never forget today, or how attractive he was, or how polite to her—though how that would affect her future when it came to men remained to be seen. They would all fall short if she compared them to Rigo.

For his part, Rigo seemed to have got over the shock of meeting her and was treating her with indulgence like a young relative recently arrived from the country.

'There's the Colosseum,' he said, pointing it out. 'Can you see it?'

And was that St Peter's Basilica? She wanted to ask, but realised he would only think her more gauche and awkward than ever. Signor Ruggiero's home in Rome was in one of the most fashionable squares and had a panoramic view of so much of the beautiful city.

'I'll draw the blinds,' he said, when she impulsively shaded her eyes to take another look. He pressed a button and it was done. He pressed another button and a tinted glass roof closed over their heads. 'Thank you,' she murmured, glad to be in the shadows again.

And now it was down to business—no more time wasted on wishing Signor Ruggiero could look at her and see her differently, someone with more class and polish than she possessed...and no flaws.

'Are you cold, Signorina Bannister?'

Try frigid.

'You're trembling,' he said.

'Just travel-weary, I expect.' By then he had pressed yet another button on the console on his desk, activating some invisible heat source.

'Travel-weary?' he murmured, and there was a faintly

amused look in his eyes. 'I forgot—you've had such a long flight.'

And it would be the same short flight home, Katie thought, knowing she would have to sharpen up with this man or be made a complete fool of. She started by putting a professional smile on her lips. 'Shall we begin?'

'Whenever you're ready,' he said, still looking at her with faint amusement.

Reaching for the thick manila envelope she had put in front of her on the desk, Katie opened it. But concern for its contents washed over her and she stopped. She had heard so many unkind things expressed in wills, and was well aware they could be used like a weapon to hurt those left behind. She hoped she wasn't the bearer of some last bitter note from Rigo Ruggiero's stepbrother.

'What are you waiting for, Signorina Bannister?'

Yes, why should she care what was in the will? She fumbled the sheets and finally managed to spread the document out in front of her. 'This is the last will and testament of—'

'Cut to the chase—we both know whose will this is.'

Rigo Ruggiero's charm had evaporated. He could change in an instant, she had discovered. It would be a foolish person who underestimated him. He had charm only when he chose to have charm.

'My time is short, Signorina Bannister.'

And you are handling this badly, his expression clearly said. She wasn't supposed to get involved. She had received this same criticism at work. It was her only failing, the senior partner had told her at her annual assessment. Deal with the facts, Ms Bannister. We are not employed to dole out tea and sympathy—and make sure you keep an accurate time sheet of every moment you spend with the client.

Even at times like these when she could be revealing

anything to Signor Ruggiero? Was she supposed to close her heart and send the bill? She had never managed to do so before, and now she stood less chance than ever. Her clock wasn't running. They should have sent a more experienced member of the firm if they wanted her to account for every second of compassion in her.

'Please move on.'

She did so with a dry throat. Even her so-called sexy voice sounded strained. There was clearly no love lost between Rigo and his stepbrother. Didn't he feel any nostalgia for his childhood? His darkening expression suggested not. She was out of place, out of step here…

Reminding herself she was merely a servant of the firm, she pulled herself together and got on with it, only to have Rigo explode with, *'Tcha!'* as the phone rang. He made her jump as he banged the table. Obviously he didn't want to be interrupted at a time like this, and as he reached for the telephone she spoke up.

'If I answer it I can put them off for you. I can say I'm your PA…'

Briefly, she thought she saw something light in his eyes, and then with a curt nod of agreement he withdrew his hand, leaving her to pick up the phone.

'Pronto?' She shot Rigo a glance. People had different ways of expressing emotion when someone close to them died. Carlo Ruggiero had been part of Rigo Ruggiero's life once—he must be feeling something, though he was hiding it well.

Refocusing on the call, Katie continued to talk in fluent Italian, and only slowly realised that Rigo was staring at her in astonishment.

'Why didn't you tell me you spoke Italian?' he said accusingly as she ended the call.

'I didn't realise it would be of any interest to you.'

He looked taken aback, but quickly recovered. 'No, you're right. Well?' he said impatiently. 'Are you going to tell me who it was?'

She managed her feelings. This was none of her business. 'It appears you have forgotten a rather important engagement…'

He jumped up immediately when she explained. Extracting a phone from his pocket, he placed a call and began to pace.

He would only break off this meeting before he found out everything for one reason and this was it. The scheme he had set up to fulfil children's dreams came ahead of his personal concerns. If taking a child around the track in his sports car was being brought forward then there must be a very good reason for it. 'Of course he can come right away,' he told his friend.

Moving out of earshot so Katie Bannister couldn't hear, he explained his schedule for the day had been thrown thanks to missing the solicitor he was due to meet at the airport—and, yes, he had found the young woman, eventually.

'A young woman?' his friend murmured with a knowing air.

'A very quiet and respectable young woman,' he emphasised, staring at the back of Katie Bannister's head. She had thick, glossy hair the same shade of honey as her eyes, but she wore it scraped back cruelly in a way that did her no favours. He refocused on his conversation and shut her out. His friend brought her back in again.

'What a disappointment for you, Rigo,' he drawled, 'but no doubt you have a plan in mind to change this young woman's way of thinking?'

Actually, no, he had no plan, and his friend's comment had left him feeling vaguely irritated. 'I'm leaving now.' He ended the call. This was not the moment to be discussing such things, and something about Signorina Bannister called for the role of protector, rather than seducer. She was far too young for him, and almost certainly a virgin—or at least incredibly inexperienced; ergo, she was not his type at all. He stowed the phone in his shirt pocket and turned back to her. 'You'll have to keep this reading on hold. I've been called away. We'll reschedule—'

'But my flight home…' she said anxiously.

'I can only apologise.'

Katie frowned. It wasn't up to her to judge the client, but this was unforgivable. Rigo Ruggiero intended to leave something as important as the reading of his stepbrother's will to race his sports car around a track. Couldn't he do that some other time? His equally arrogant friend hadn't been prepared to tell her much more, but she gathered that was the plan. 'There's no need to apologise,' she said coldly, remembering the senior partner's words. 'After all, you're paying for my time—'

'Plus ça change,' he interrupted and his expression registered nothing more than resigned acceptance of the way of things.

Now she was insulted. Her motive in coming to Rome had not been money. The fact that she had come here to fulfil his stepbrother's last request didn't matter to him at all, apparently.

He saw this change in her and emphasized, 'This is something I cannot miss—'

'And I cannot miss my flight,' she said, standing up.

'You can change it—'

'I'm not sure I can—'

'Why not?'

Because she would have to buy a new ticket—an expense that would mean nothing to this man and that in their present parlous state her firm probably wouldn't reimburse. She had bills to pay—and the prospect of no job to return to ahead of her.

She had tried so hard to strike the right tone and be professional, but she was growing increasingly agitated as she faced Rigo Ruggiero across the desk. Like it or not, they were in conflict now. 'Couldn't you change your appointment?' she suggested hesitantly.

'No.'

'But you are eager to get this over with?' she reminded him. And not put off by a drive around the racetrack with the boys.

'I assure you I am every bit as eager as I was before, but now I must go—'

'Shall I wait for you?'

Already halfway to the door, he spun around. 'Make yourself at home.'

Tension had propelled her to breaking point. She might be a small-town solicitor, and dull as ditchwater if you compared her to the blistering glamour of a man like this, but she wasn't anyone's doormat. 'Signor Ruggiero, please,' she called, chasing after him. 'This just can't wait—'

'And neither can my appointment,' he called back to her from the door. 'You must be content—'

Content?

As he spoke one strong, tanned hand flexed impatiently on the door handle. 'I will return as quickly as I can—'

'But my flight—'

'Book another flight.'

The next sound she heard was the sound of the door slamming on his private quarters.

Great, Katie thought, subsiding. She was going to miss her flight.

So what would she do? She would have to stay in Rome. But since the fire privacy was all-important. She'd never stayed away from home since the fire. She had never risked anyone seeing her scars. What if a hotel maid or a porter walked in on her by accident? The thought of it made her blood run cold.

She wasn't ready for this—maybe she never would be. And where would she stay? Could she even afford to stay in a city as expensive as Rome on her limited budget?

'*Ciao, bella.*'

On the point of tears, she swung around clumsily, almost crashing into the fabulous desk as Rigo Ruggiero stormed out of the apartment in a cloud of testosterone and expensive cologne. *Ciao, bella?* He must have mistaken her for someone else.

But her nipples were impressed, Katie realised with astonishment. Well, she could dream, couldn't she? *Ciao, bella...*

Her sensible self lost no time telling her she should be concerned at these unmistakeable signs of arousal, because Rigo Ruggiero roused more than awe inside her, he roused lust.

And frustration.

And anger.

He inspired that too, because this just wasn't fair. How long did it take to race around a track? Was she supposed to sit here waiting indefinitely for him?

She would go and find a cheap hotel, Katie concluded, putting the will back in its envelope. Wandering to the window, she took a last look out, debating whether to book a flight today, tomorrow—or next week, maybe? Who the hell knew? She was of no importance to Signor Ruggiero and had been dismissed. Far from being impatient to know the contents of his stepbrother's will, as he had told her, he had proved himself all too easily distracted. The words *play* and *boy* had never made more sense to her. Rigo Ruggiero was like a film star—all top show. He was a man with too much money and not enough to occupy his time.

Staring down at the road a dizzying distance below, she watched his sleek red car pull out smoothly into the chaos of Roman traffic. Everyone gave way for him, of course. But not her, Katie determined, firming her jaw. Not that she'd ever get the chance. But then her dreamy self came to the fore and she wondered, if she had looked different—more glamorous, more appealing—would Rigo have taken her to the track with him?

And why should she care? It was time to stop daydreaming and start making plans.

An open ticket home was the best thing, Katie decided, and then the moment this business was concluded she could fly home. Rigo Ruggiero might have consigned her to the pigeonhole marked miscellaneous, along with all the other women who, for reasons of age, or inferior looks, had failed to meet his exacting standards, but even in her dreams she didn't want to spend any more time than she had to with a man so self-absorbed he'd put a drive around a racetrack ahead of the reading of his stepbrother's will.

Which naturally accounted for her heart trying to beat its way out of her chest. Who was she trying to fool? Katie wondered as the phone rang again. She looked across the room. Where were the snooty staff she'd had to get past at his office? Had he sacked them all? Surely a man like Rigo Ruggiero had a PA who could sort out his appointments and answer his phone? But if he had, there was no sign of him or her.

The phone continued to peal until finally she gave in and picked it up. *'Pronto?'*

'Signorina Bannister?'

No. A Hollywood film star, she felt like telling Rigo Ruggiero at that moment. *'Sì,'* she said instead, forcing an agreeable note into her voice.

'I feel bad.'

Oh, no! She pulled a face and somehow managed to sound pleasantly surprised at the same time. 'Oh...?'

'You should make the most of your time in Rome.'

Really? 'But I'll be leaving shortly,' she pointed out, waiting in vain for the surge of relief those words should bring.

'Have you booked another flight yet?'

Ah, so he couldn't wait to get rid of her. 'I was about to—'

'Well, don't. Not until I get back.'

Commands now? Did she work for him? 'But, Signor Ruggiero, I'm not equipped to stay over—'

'Not equipped? What's your problem? Buy whatever you need and charge it to me.'

What? 'I couldn't possibly!' Katie exclaimed with affront— though she did allow her imagination a five-second trolley dash through Rome's most expensive store with Rigo Ruggiero's credit card clutched tightly in her hand. 'I don't have a hotel.'

'A hotel? Don't be ridiculous. I have seven bedrooms.'

Now she really was too shocked to speak.

'Signorina Bannister? Are you still there?'

'Yes,' Katie managed hoarsely.

'Don't forget we still have business to conclude, you and I. I expect you there on my return. How hard can it be?' he added in a more soothing tone. 'My penthouse has a roof garden accessed through the staircase in the hallway, as well as an outdoor pool with the finest views over Rome you'll ever see. There's a resident chef on call at the press of a button, and an entertainment centre with a gym attached to the spa. Use the place like your own. And don't forget—be there when I return. Oh, and in the meantime—answer any incoming calls and make a note of them, would you?'

Katie was still choking out words of protest when Rigo cut the line.

CHAPTER FOUR

THE telephone receiver was in serious danger of connecting with the plate-glass window. And she thought she knew everything there was to know about controlling feelings? Did Rigo seriously expect her to remain on standby at his command? He must think everyone lived the same racy billionaire lifestyle he did. Some people had work to do.

Yes…like answering his phone, Katie concluded as it rang again. Glaring at the receiver, she walked over to the cradle, pressed a few buttons and switched it to record. Now she could take stock. She could fret all she liked, but she *was* going to miss her plane, meaning she *would* have to stay another night in Rome. But not here. Not with Rigo Ruggiero. Not in a million years.

She didn't want to panic anyone, so her first call must be to the office. She would give them a carefully edited version of events. That done, she would book into a reasonably priced hotel—if she could find such a thing in Rome. Then she must do some shopping—toiletries and nightclothes, if nothing else. And if Rigo Ruggiero wanted to hear the reading of his stepbrother's will and receive the package she had brought with her, he could damn well come and find her.

* * *

Katie booked into a respectable hotel, taking a compact room on the fourth floor with a view of the air-conditioning units. But she had everything she needed: a clean bed and a functioning bathroom, as well as a desk, an easy chair and a television. Best of all, there were quiet spaces in the lobby where she could meet up with Rigo when he found her. She was confident he would find her; that was what men like him were good at.

And now what?

She had paced the three strides by six it took to mark out the floor of her room, and was left facing the fact that she was alone in the raciest and most fashionable city on earth...a city she longed to explore. So, she could sit here in her hotel room, or be really adventurous and sit in the lobby.

She could always watch TV...

In Rome?

What about her shopping? There had to be a chain store close to the hotel.

Katie asked the concierge, who directed her to the Via del Corso, which he said was one of the busiest shopping streets in town. It certainly was, she discovered, though it bore no resemblance to any shopping street back home. It was so glamorous and buzzy she just stood and stared when she found it, until people jostled her and she was forced to move along.

So now what? Now she was a tourist, and she was enjoying every minute of it. Work seemed a million miles away...

After a moment's hesitation, she took a deep breath and plunged right in.

To Katie's surprise she loved every moment of the chaotic bustle, and hearing the lyrical Italian language being spoken all around her more than made up for the mayhem of the crowded streets. She had learned to love Italian at the music conservatoire she had attended, in what seemed to her like another lifetime now. Determined to brush all melancholy thoughts away, she told herself that she would never get another opportunity like this and should be savouring every moment so she could store away the memories to share with the girls in the office.

She began with some serious window shopping, which involved frantically trying to work out how many fantasy purchases she could fit into her fantasy wardrobe, not to mention how much fantasy designer luggage would be required to transport all these fantasy purchases home. But there was one adventure she could afford, Katie realised as she walked along, and that was drinking coffee at a pavement café like a real Roman.

She would be mad not to enjoy the shade of late afternoon, Katie convinced herself, feeling a little nervous as she eyed up a likely café. There were a few free seats, and, with all the new scents and sounds around her and the clear blue sky like an umbrella overhead, the temptation to linger and soak it all in was irresistible.

If she didn't do it now she never would. Everyone had their shoulders thrown back in the warmth of the sun, and were talking loudly—as much with gestures as with their voices. This way of life intrigued her. It was so different from seeing people with their backs hunched against an icy wind and she wanted to be part of it, even if it was only for an afternoon. She wanted to let her hair down and be as uninhibited as all the other girls her age, who looked so fashionable and sassy in their street clothes.

Let her hair down? Yes. She might even unbutton her jacket, Katie decided in a wry moment of abandon. Spotting an empty table in a prime position, she targeted it. Why not?

Shouldn't she make the most of this short trip and live a little while she had the chance?

The handsome, dark-eyed waiter who brought Katie the menu was quite a flirt. He repeated the old cliché that while she was in Rome she must do as the Romans did—though the look in his eyes suggested that might be a step too far for her. When her cheeks pinked up he pursued a different line, suggesting *gelato alla vaniglia* as an alternative—making vanilla ice cream sound like the most decadent food on earth. He advised that this should be accompanied by a strong black coffee and some iced water to help the sweetness down.

Katie thanked him in Italian. *'Ringrazie molto, signore.'*

'Ah, you speak Italian…!' Elaborate gestures accompanied this exclamation, and then he continued to stare at her with deep pools of longing in his puppy-dog eyes. 'Are you quite sure that's *all* I can help you with, *signorina*?' he murmured passionately.

'Quite sure, thank you.'

Katie smiled. She knew the waiter was only joking but, looking around, she had gathered that was the Roman way—every man was duty-bound to flirt. 'However,' she said, deciding to play the waiter at his own game, 'there is one thing…'

'Sì…?' Hope revived, the man dipped lower.

'May I have my coffee now, please?'

'Certamente, signorina,' he said, affecting disappointment, but as he left he gave Katie a wink as if to say he'd recognised a fellow tease.

She was really beginning to enjoy herself, Katie realised, eyes sparkling with fun as the waiter walked away. She hadn't flirted with a man since before the accident and then never seriously. In fact, this was the most excitement she'd ever had. Rome was proving to be everything it was reputed to be— magical, romantic, awe-inspiring…a city of adventure, and it had unleashed something in her.

Let's just hope it wasn't her reckless, inner self, Katie mused, because that fantasy Katie was far safer locked away. Thinking of Rigo—which she was doing rather a lot lately—it wouldn't be wise to push the boundaries too far on this first attempt to live her dream.

A shadow fell over her table. A ripple of awareness ran down her spine.

No.

It couldn't be—

'Signorina Bannister.'

'Rigo!' Lurching to her feet, she quickly sat down again. Why should she feel so guilty? But she did. 'You're the last person I expected to see—'

'Clearly.'

Tipping designer shades down his nose, he shot a glance at the waiter. Had he heard something of their conversation? Well, if he had he'd got the wrong idea. Rigo's hackles were so far up he was practically snarling. 'So, this is what you get up to while I'm away?' he demanded when the waiter disappeared inside the café.

'Did you enjoy your drive around the track?' she countered pleasantly.

'I thought I asked you to wait for me at the penthouse?'

'I didn't know how long you would be—'

'I also thought you had a plane to catch,' he interrupted. 'You were in a tearing hurry to leave, as I remember—'

'But how can I before I've read the will? And I missed my plane.' She resisted the temptation to add, thanks to you. Leaning on her hand, she stared up and from somewhere found the courage to hold his stare.

Rigo visibly bridled again as the waiter returned with her coffee. What was the poor waiter supposed to do? She'd ordered coffee and he was perfectly within his rights to bring it. And how dared Rigo question her actions when he had left her on the flimsiest of pretexts and for an unspecified length of time?

But as they still had business to complete her reasonable self conceded that it might be better to build bridges. 'Would you like to join me?' She pointed to an empty chair.

Rigo pulled out two chairs. 'As you can see, I am not alone…'

Now she noticed his companion was the beautiful young blonde in the magazine. The girl had been shopping and was making her way towards them, weighed down by countless carrier bags. The café was obviously a prearranged meeting place.

Every man turned to watch as the young girl threaded her way through the tables. Katie couldn't blame them, the girl was gorgeous—especially when she lifted the carrier bags on high to avoid hitting anyone with them, revealing even more perfectly toned thigh.

Composing her face, Katie determined to love this young woman for the short time she would have to know her—if only so as not to appear small-minded and deadly jealous, though this resolution took a nosedive when the girl draped herself over Rigo.

'Rigo, il mio amore,' she pouted, tugging at his resistant arm, 'sì sara lunga?'

Having asked whether he would be much longer, she turned her luminous stare on Katie.

Katie smiled, or tried her very hardest to.

After taking full inventory of Katie, Rigo's companion appeared satisfied and risked a sultry smile.

No doubt having concluded I'm no threat, Katie reasoned.

'Antonia,' Rigo protested in a weary voice, 'please try to remember that Signorina Bannister is here in Rome on business.'

Rigo was defending her? She *had* gone up in the world, Katie thought wryly, trying not to mind when Rigo settled his young companion into the chair next to her own.

'Don't worry, I know when I'm not wanted,' Antonia responded sulkily, refusing to sit down now she had deposited her bags. 'I don't want to be here while you're talking business—'

'Oh, please, don't go on account of me…' Katie seized the opportunity to stand up. 'I was just going anyway—'

'No, you weren't,' Rigo argued. 'You've barely started your coffee.'

Katie's instinctive reaction was to look down at Rigo's hand on her arm. Could he feel her trembling beneath his touch?

'And you sit down too,' he instructed Antonia, lifting his hand away from Katie. 'What's wrong with you both?'

Where to begin? Katie thought, feeling like the poor relation. But Rigo had made it impossible for her to leave without appearing rude, and so reluctantly she sat down again.

Only Rigo appeared relaxed as silence stretched between them. With Antonia sulking and Rigo paying neither of them much attention, this was uncomfortable. 'So…you found me?' Katie mumbled self-consciously. She wasn't the best conversationalist at the best of times—and this was hardly that. As Rigo turned to her she was vaguely aware that the waiter was serving more coffee, as well as a soda and a piece of delicious ice-cream cake known as *semifredo* for Antonia.

'Found you?' Rigo's sexy lips pressed down. 'It appears so,' he agreed, lowering a fringe of jet-black lashes over his emerald eyes. 'I guess it must be fate.'

His direct stare made her hand shake and she quickly replaced her coffee-cup in the saucer before she spilled it.

'Of course,' he added, 'if you will choose to walk down the most popular shopping street in Rome…'

His wry look plus Antonia's raspberry and vanilla scent

was a lethal combination, Katie realised, finding her gaze drawn to his sexy mouth. 'Er—yes…'

'And here was I, thinking you were back at the penthouse answering my calls—' his lips pressed down '—while all the time you were out shopping.'

By now her cheeks must be luminous crimson, Katie realised, glancing at Antonia, who, having decided to stay, was wolfing down cake as if calories never stuck to her thighs. 'I awarded myself a break—'

'I applaud your initiative, Signorina Bannister.'

A bone-melting stare over the rim of his coffee-cup accompanied this assurance.

Play with fire and you are likely to get burned, Katie reminded herself, managing to slop her own coffee over the table.

She reached for a wad of paper napkins, but Signor Ruggiero got there first.

'Allow me,' he insisted. 'Tell me, Signorina Bannister,' he said, angling his stubble-shaded chin to slant a stare directly into her eyes, 'should I want to employ you, do you think I could trust you to resist the lure of shopping in Rome?'

Was he serious? Did he think she could endure this level of tension every day? 'If you wanted to employ me, Signor Ruggiero, I should have to warn you, I'm not free—'

'Rigo,' he reminded her. 'Ah, well,' he murmured, lips pressing down in mock-regret, 'I shall just have to find a way to live with the disappointment.' He glanced at his watch. 'We should be getting back to finish our business. What have you done about your flight?'

'I've bought an open ticket.'

'Ah, good,' he said, relaxing back. 'In that case we're in no hurry, and you have no excuse not to join me and Antonia for dinner tonight.'

Dinner? Tonight? With Antonia and Rigo? It would take

too long to list all her objections. To give herself time to come up with a watertight excuse, she smiled as she pretended to consider the offer. While she was doing that, and with exquisitely bad timing, the same testosterone-fuelled waiter placed an enormous dish of ice cream in front of her.

'Or perhaps you would prefer to eat something less wholesome tonight?' Rigo challenged, flashing a vicious stare on the hapless man. 'Ice cream, for instance?'

This was ridiculous, Katie concluded. Men were ridiculous. The waiter was still pulling those funny faces at her, while Rigo was taking the man's interest in her for real. And now both men were glaring at each other.

Because of her?

How preposterous!

CHAPTER FIVE

THIS could only happen in Rome, Katie concluded. She knew the waiter would run a mile if she so much as showed the slightest interest in him. As far as Rigo was concerned, it was slightly different. He was the leader of the pack and brooked no competition, whether false or genuine. No one looked at a woman when Rigo Ruggiero was with her; that was Rigo's law. But he had to understand she wasn't his possession. She was an independent woman of independent means—even if those means were somewhat slim compared to his—and she was trying to enjoy her short time in Rome…or she had been up to a few minutes ago. 'Thank you for the offer of dinner,' she said, standing up, 'but I have decided to have a lazy evening by myself at the hotel—'

'The Russie?' Rigo frowned as he mentioned arguably the most exclusive hotel in Rome and probably the only one that registered on his radar.

Katie had to curb her smile when she mentioned the name of the hotel where she was actually staying. 'I can assure you, it's perfectly respectable,' she said, seeing Rigo's and Antonia's reaction to the name.

'I have no doubt,' Rigo said, looking less than convinced.

When Antonia yawned and said she might as well go home

if Rigo was going to ignore her Katie seized the opportunity to suggest they reschedule their meeting for the following morning at nine. There was still plenty of sightseeing she wanted to do. 'If nine isn't too early for you?' She tried very hard not to look at Antonia.

'Nine o'clock is perfect for me,' Rigo assured her, 'but at my penthouse, not your hotel.'

As he stared at her she found the way he had seized back control arousing. But as she had never experienced this sort of power play before...

Slipping on the designer shades, he stood up so that now he was towering over her. 'And this time you shall have my undivided attention.'

Why did that sound like such a threat?

It took her entirely by surprise when he brought her hand to his lips and kissed the back of it. The touch of those warm, firm lips was an incendiary device sending streams of sensation to invade her body and blank her mind.

'Before you go, Signorina Bannister—'

She snatched her hand away. 'Yes?' She tried prim. She tried haughty. And failed miserably with both. Haughty was so foreign to her and, with those wicked eyes staring deep into her own eyes, how on earth was she supposed to fake prim?

'This is most remiss of me,' Rigo said, turning to Antonia and indicating that she should stand up too.

'What is?' Katie tensed, immediately on guard.

'I should have introduced you two to each other—'

'Which I made impossible,' Antonia cut across him to Katie's surprise, 'because I had to guzzle that delicious cake before I did another thing.'

Cake she could understand, but introductions?

'Indeed,' Rigo agreed patiently, brushing a strand of errant blonde hair out of Antonia's eyes. 'Signorina Bannister, I would like to introduce you to my spoiled little sister, Antonia…'

Losing her pout, the girl bounded round the table to give Katie a hug. 'Welcome to Rome, Signorina Bannister.' And then she found her pout again. 'Rigo never lets me meet anyone interesting.'

Interesting? Katie was so shocked she remained unresponsive for a moment. Well, this was something to report back to the girls in the office, as was the hug, and the kiss on both cheeks from Antonia. Having hugged the young girl back, she thought this had to be the perfect example of the attraction of opposites. Katie couldn't imagine there were many quiet, country secretaries in the world Antonia inhabited, and there certainly weren't any vivacious little pop-star lookalikes in hers.

Now that the barrier of believing Antonia was Rigo's girlfriend had been removed, Katie was surprised to find that conversation between them flowed easily and Antonia soon persuaded her to sit down again. Being a willowy blonde, Antonia didn't look a bit like her tough, dark-haired brother, which meant she must be the child born when Rigo's father had married Carlo's mother. He had no trouble with this relationship, so why did he hate his stepbrother? She really should pay more attention to the editorial in gossip magazines.

'So, do you really have everything you need?' Antonia prompted, giving Katie a meaningful look. 'Now that my wicked brother has kept you here in Rome, you must need to go shopping. It never occurs to you, Rigo,' she added, turning to him, 'that other people don't have a home in every city.' And when he shrugged carelessly, Antonia added, 'I bet poor Katie doesn't even have a decent toothbrush with her—'

'Well, as it happens,' Katie interrupted wryly, getting the gist of this conversation, 'I do need to do some shopping for…essentials.'

'Lucky for you, then, that you have an expert on hand!' Antonia exclaimed, satisfied that her ruse had worked. 'You'll definitely need toothpaste and a hairbrush, and all sorts of boring stuff…'

Katie was relieved Rigo hadn't seen Antonia's theatrical wink.

'Are you offering to take Katie shopping?' he said, frowning.

'Could you spare your sister?' Katie suggested, thinking what fun it could be.

'Anyone who can keep Antonia entertained for an hour or two…' His voice faded when he noticed Antonia looking at him and Katie thought Antonia's smile had faded too. 'I'd love to go shopping with you,' she said, taking pity on the young girl, at which point Antonia quickly brightened.

'But don't forget—dinner at eight,' Rigo reminded them as the two girls collected up their things.

'Really, I'm perfectly happy eating in my room at the hotel,' Katie assured him, sending an apologetic smile Antonia's way.

'I wouldn't hear of it,' Rigo insisted with a decisive shake of his head. 'Antonia is right. You must allow me to make up for leaving you so abruptly this afternoon—'

'I *must*?' The challenge flew from Katie's blunt mouth before she could stop it, which made Antonia laugh.

'It seems to me, you have met your match, Rigo,' she told her brother in Italian.

Rigo didn't look nearly so pleased and Katie took note of the cold look in his eyes. Fortunately, she had the perfect excuse. 'It's very kind of you, but I don't have anything to wear.'

'Antonia is taking you shopping.'

'Yes, for a toothbrush.'

And now Antonia was looking at her as if she had gone completely mad.

'I really don't need anything special to wear for a night in at my hotel…' Seeing Antonia's disappointment, Katie knew she had to backtrack. 'But I do need a really good toothbrush…'

'And I know every toothbrush shop in Rome,' Antonia assured her, smiling again now she had got her shopping companion back onto the right track.

It was easy to see why Antonia was spoiled, Katie concluded. Antonia had her brother's charm, only with Antonia that charm didn't have an off switch. But there was another look in Antonia's eyes—a defensive look, almost as if the young girl was used to being let down.

'And if we should see some lovely dresses on the way?' Antonia pressed, glancing anxiously at her brother.

Katie tensed. Shopping for clothes was an absolute no. What if Antonia saw her scars? What if, in her enthusiasm, Antonia burst into the changing room and screamed? She couldn't do that to such a vulnerable young girl. She couldn't risk it. She had to renege on her promise, even with Antonia smiling hopefully at her.

She would have to tread very carefully here, Katie realised with concern.

She was barely given time to worry before Rigo offered her a way out. 'Buy something nice for both of you,' he said, glancing at Katie as he pressed a pile of money into Antonia's hand.

'Oh, no.' Katie held up her hands. This was something she drew the line at. 'I couldn't possibly accept your money—'

'But I can,' Antonia said, quickly securing the wad in her super-sized handbag.

'Please,' Rigo insisted. 'It's the very least I can do after treating you so badly, Signorina Bannister—'

'The very least,' Antonia assured him with a frown.

'So…dinner at eight?' he said, turning to Katie. 'Don't forget—I'll pick you up at your hotel.'

This was a man to whom no one had ever dared to say no, Katie concluded. 'I'll be eating in my room tonight,' she reminded him pleasantly.

'After you go shopping with me,' Antonia insisted.

'Of course,' Katie reassured Antonia with a smile. She was beginning to feel like the bland filling in a particularly glamorous sandwich. 'I can't wait to go shopping…for a really good toothbrush,' she added for Rigo's benefit, 'and I look forward to concluding our business tomorrow morning,' she finished with absolute honesty. How much more of this high-octane challenge could she take? To make the point that she wasn't the type to take advantage, as the waiter threaded nimbly past she picked up their bill from his tray.

Which Rigo stole from her hand with a warning glance.

The shopping trip with Antonia exceeded Katie's wildest expectations.

Did it come any wilder? She had no idea how to rein in Antonia's enthusiasm—this was shopping on a heroic scale. Just as she had anticipated, Antonia ignored her insistence that Katie only needed a toothbrush and, as everything in the shops was so stylishly arranged…

But Katie knew she'd reached her boundary when Antonia called her over to look in one particular window. Katie had never seen so many exclusive boutiques in one place and had been lagging behind. The specialist shops they were browsing now sold everything under the sun and more besides—things that should only come out at night, like garments of a frilly nature, for example…

Katie stood awestruck, taking in the breathtaking display. Cobweb-fine lace and slinky satin vied with cotton so delicate you could see through it—and many of the items were trimmed with eye-catching diamanté and pearl. 'Oh, no, I couldn't,' she said when Antonia tried to persuade her to go with her into the shop. 'You go in if you want to,' Katie said, hanging back.

'Not without you,' Antonia insisted, taking hold of Katie's arm. And before Katie knew what was happening Antonia had marched her into the shop, announcing, 'It's time you spoiled yourself.'

Antonia immediately summoned assistants over to help them. 'Not with Rigo's money,' Katie said, determined to resist Antonia's enthusiasm.

'But you've got your own money, haven't you?'

How to say, yes, but I need it for bills? Though she could do with some pyjamas for tonight, Katie conceded, mouth agape as she stared around. Did people wear these things?

'Well, that's a start,' Antonia approved when Katie suggested that perhaps pyjama trousers and a vest to sleep in that night might be a good idea.

What the assistants brought them was the furthest thing from Katie's mind, but as she handled the delicate garments her longing for them grew. They were in such glorious colours—turquoise, cerise, lemon and lavender trimmed with baby-pink. It went without saying that she would never find anything like this at home.

Did she have to wear winceyette all the time? Katie wondered, staring at her plain face in the mirror. As no one else was going to see the satin shorts and revealing strappy top she liked, surely it wouldn't hurt to buy a set…or two?

Giving herself the excuse she wouldn't risk offending Antonia, she asked the assistant to wrap them up.

'And what about these?' Antonia cut in, pointing out some racy underwear.

'Oh, no…' Shaking her head, Katie blushed furiously, knowing she would never have the opportunity to wear it. She had only seen underwear like that in magazines before.

'You can't wear white cotton all your life,' Antonia observed, staring frankly into Katie's eyes.

'How do you…' Katie's words froze on her lips. Was she that obvious?

'They are expensive,' Antonia continued thoughtfully as she studied the set, 'so you really should try them on before you buy them.'

Alarm bells rang in Katie's head. She had pushed all her hang-ups to the back of her mind, she realised as Antonia waited for her to do the obvious and ask to use the changing room. 'No,' she said firmly, knowing she had to get out of this somehow. She'd say she'd changed her mind. 'There's no need…'

'Oh, well, if you're sure,' Antonia said, completely mis-understanding her. 'We'll take these too, please—'

Katie didn't speak up quickly enough and as she watched Antonia handing the racy garments to the assistant they were being wrapped up before she knew it.

She could have stopped this at any time, Katie admitted to herself, but the bare truth was, she didn't want to stop it. She wanted to take the underwear back to her hotel where she could try it on with no one seeing her scars, and pretend.

To make matters worse, the assistant, having secured Katie's purchases in fuchsia-pink tissue paper, was lowering them reverently into a pale pink carrier bag decorated with the logo of a naked woman seated in a champagne glass. 'Very subtle,' Katie commented wryly as the two girls left the shop. She loved the bag, but part of her wished the logo didn't have to be on both sides.

Linking arms with her, Antonia gave Katie a squeeze. 'We're going to buy a few more things for you, and then I'm under

strict instructions from Rigo to put you in a taxi back to your
hotel— Oh, look,' she broke off excitedly, 'there he is now…'

Katie gasped to see Rigo coming out of a menswear shop
across the street. He was just pushing his sunglasses back on
his nose and spotted them right away. He came over. How
could she hide the carrier bag?

He stood in front of them, making every part of her sing
with awareness. But worst of all he was staring at the brazen
proof that her latest purchase had not been a toothbrush.

'I trust you girls found everything you needed in the
shops?' he said, straight-faced.

She could read the subtext and blushed violently. 'Yes,
thank you,' she said, raising her head to meet his gaze. 'And,
as you can see, I'm carrying some of Antonia's bags for her.'

Rigo's amused stare called her a liar.

CHAPTER SIX

WHEN Rigo left them Katie and Antonia continued their shopping, but there was a *frisson* of understanding between them now. Neither girl commented on the change Rigo had made to their day, but they were aware of how profoundly he affected them, each in their own way. It brought them closer, though it took a little time when he'd gone to recapture the rhythm of easy friendship they had established. When they did Katie almost forgot to buy her toothbrush.

The fun of being with someone as non-judgemental and as warm as Antonia was so unexpected Katie threw herself into the expedition with enthusiasm, and by the time she returned to her small hotel room there were lots more packages. Antonia had shown Katie the best shopping in Rome—small boutiques hidden in side-streets around the Piazza Novona and Campo di Fiori, and other places that were well off the regular tourist beat, and when they both finally admitted defeat, they had more coffee and ice cream at a café on Via Acaia, where Katie thought the lemon cream or *crema al limone* and the scrunchy chocolate *stracciatella* were to die for. She insisted before they parted on buying Antonia a special little gift to say thank you to Rigo's sister for being so kind to her.

It was obvious Antonia adored her brother. To hear Antonia talk you would think Rigo was a saint—but, as Antonia appeared to be the chief recipient of Rigo's generosity, Antonia could hardly be called impartial.

Katie smiled, remembering Antonia's pleasure when Katie bought her a small aqua leather-backed journal. To prove the point, Antonia had started scribbling in it right away, and when she secured the small gilt lock she had exclaimed, 'Thank you so much for today, Katie…'

And when it was she who had everything to thank Antonia for…

Katie's heart went out to the teenager, who on the face of it appeared to have everything a girl of Antonia's age could possibly want, but she suspected all Antonia really wanted was a little of her brother's time.

Time. That was what so many rich and successful people lacked, Katie mused, moving the faded curtain back to stare out of the window. They had none to spare when it came to those closest to them.

'We are friends, aren't we?' Antonia had demanded fiercely when they parted. Whatever she thought of Antonia's brother Katie had put to one side, promising Antonia they would be friends for ever.

After a rocky start it had been a good day, Katie reflected, turning back to look at her purchases spread out on the bed. Now her smile was one of disbelief. What on earth had possessed her? Antonia was the simple answer. Thanks to Rigo's sister, it was goodbye brown, hello colour! And in the open-air market Katie had spotted a silk dress swinging on its hanger in the breeze. In a bright gypsy-rose print, it had long sleeves and a short, flirty skirt, and there was a sexy cut-out panel at the midriff—one of the few places where she could afford to show some skin. With the option of trying it on taken away from her, she hadn't been able to resist. She had added a couple of tops and a shawl to her haul, as well as a pair of jeans—something she had never owned before.

'And trainers,' Antonia had insisted, determined that Katie should update her image. 'For someone who is only twenty-five, you dress too old,' she had commented with all the blunt assurance of a teenager.

And that was me told, Katie reflected, smiling as she left the bedroom to enter her small *ensuite* bathroom. She had treated herself to some foam bath too. It was a cheap way to turn even the most basic of bathrooms into a better place. And now there was nothing more for her to do but soak and dream until she felt like ringing downstairs for Room Service.

Bliss.

Now he remembered why it was so long since he had treated Antonia to dinner. Nothing was quite right for his teenage sister. Their table could have been better—it was too near the door. Their fellow diners were too stuffy—meaning most of them were over twenty-five and had brushed their hair before coming out. She sniffed everything that arrived at their table with suspicion as if three Michelin stars was no guarantee at all, and to top it off she ordered chips with ketchup on the side, leaving everything else on her plate.

But his worst crime, apparently, was *abandoning* Katie in Rome on her first night in the eternal city.

'Katie?'

'Signorina Bannister insisted I call her Katie,' his sister informed him smugly as he raised a brow.

'May I remind you that Signorina Bannister is on a business trip and will shortly be returning home? She was invited to join us tonight, but she refused. And that's an end of it, Antonia.'

And might well have been, had he not felt his conscience prick.

His sister lost no time in turning that scratch into an open wound. 'Do you know where she's staying?' Antonia demanded with her customary dramatic emphasis. '*How* can you leave Katie in a place like that? Can you *imagine* what the restaurant is *like*?'

Yes, he could, unfortunately.

And so the rant went on until he couldn't face another mouthful. Laying down his cutlery, he demanded, 'What do you suggest I do, Antonia?'

Antonia appeared to be studying the menu, and he imagined she was choosing a pudding until she exclaimed, 'A picnic!'

Before he could stop her she called a waiter over.

'Take it to Katie—deliver it,' she begged him, clutching his wrist in her excitement as the waiter hurried away with the order.

'Don't be so ridiculous—'

'You don't even have to see her—'

'I have no time for this nonsense, Antonia,' he snapped impatiently, shaking her off.

'You never have time,' she flared. 'Katie gave me a whole afternoon of her time, which is more than you ever do.' Her voice was rising and people were staring at the small drama as it unfolded. 'Why can't you do something different, for once?'

'I do something different every day, Antonia. It's called business. It's what keeps you in the style to which you're accustomed.'

Thrusting back her chair, his sister took her performance to its ultimate conclusion: The Dramatic Exit. 'Well, if you won't take the picnic to Katie, I will,' she declared, storming off.

They had the attention of the whole restaurant now. As Antonia stalked away he stood up, politely murmuring an apology to those people closest to him. They should be glad of the free entertainment, he concluded as strangers exchanged knowing looks.

He caught up with Antonia at the door. 'Stop this, Antonia. You're drawing attention to yourself—'

'Oh, no!' she gasped theatrically, clutching her chest.

'I will not allow you to walk the streets of Rome alone at night—'

'That's why you must take the picnic to Katie.'

The waiter chose this moment to bring out the hamper—to a touching soundtrack of Antonia's inconsolable sobs. 'Have you no shame?' Rigo murmured, realising this was a ploy Antonia had contrived to get her own way.

'None,' his sister whispered back triumphantly.

Pressing money into the man's hand, he thanked him for his trouble. Then he escorted Antonia outside. Bringing out a handkerchief, he mopped her eyes. 'Stop crying immediately,' he insisted. 'Acting or not, you know I cannot bear to see you cry. If you're so concerned about Signorina Bannister's diet, I *will* deliver this hamper. But not before I see you safely home.'

He thought his voice had been quite stern, but he could have sworn there was a smile on Antonia's face as he helped her into the car.

Katie had put on her new dress, and after examining it from every angle in the full-length mirror had reassured herself that everything she might want to hide was hidden. It was the perfect dress for the perfect night out in Rome. Not that she was going anywhere, but there was no limit to her dream. In fact the dream was so real she had put her shawl and bag on the bed, as if all she had to do was snatch them up last minute before leaving the room.

In reality her skin prickled with apprehension just at the thought. She might be wearing her new dress, but she was frightened to leave the room wearing it.

She performed an experimental twirl, loving the way the silk felt against her skin. There wasn't room for much of a twirl, because the hotel room was very small. She had no complaints—it was functional and clean, which was all she needed.

But Rome was waiting for her outside—and tomorrow she was going home...

Moving back to the window, she stood a little to one side, staring out at the busy street scene far below. There was an open-topped tour bus that stopped right outside the hotel, and she could see people chatting to each other as they waited to board. Across the road was a family-oriented pizzeria with a neon sign. That looked fun too. Perhaps they would have room for one later...

Stop, Katie told herself firmly, pressing back against the wall. It was one thing buying into the pretence of going out and something else when she started to believe it might happen. But pretending had been fun. She had even styled her hair a number of different ways—up and down—but she had forgotten how thick and glossy even boring brown hair could be when it was washed, conditioned and blown dry with more than her usual care and even for a fantasy night out she wouldn't want to look too obvious. Her everyday style was safest, she had concluded. Over the years she had perfected the technique of brushing her hair straight back before twisting it tightly and securing it with a single tortoiseshell pin.

But she wouldn't change a thing about the dress, Katie mused, smoothing her palms over the cool silk. She eased her neck, imagining Rigo at her side...or perhaps behind her with his hands resting on her shoulders. She would lean against him…relax against him, until he dipped his head and kissed her neck as he murmured that he loved her…

She held the image in her heart for a moment, before opening her eyes and facing reality. Rigo was eating dinner with Antonia, after which he would go home to bed.

Antonia had so much to give, Katie reflected, but her brother had no time to take anything from anyone, because Rigo was too busy driving forward…

Rigo…

Leaning back against the wall again, she closed her eyes. He would look like a god tonight. She imagined him wearing a dark tailored suit with crisp white shirt and discreet gold cuff-links. The elegant look would show off his tan, his rugged strength and the power of his commanding person-ality. His hair would be freshly washed with thick, inky black waves lapping his brow and his cheekbones. He had the thickest, strongest hair she had ever seen, and though Rigo's grooming would be impeccable he would still carry that air of danger that made him irresistible, and like a magnet he would draw the gaze of every person in the room.

And she still wasn't going out, Katie told herself bluntly, opening her eyes as she pulled away from the wall. And whichever way she looked at it dreams could never compete with the reality of Rigo.

No, but dreams were safe, Katie's sensible self reminded her. With dreams there were no complications, no embarrass-ing moments, no…

Nothing.

But…

The mini-bar was full of chocolate, so it wasn't all bad.

* * *

He'd taken Antonia home and then gone back to the pent-house to change into jeans and a casual shirt before setting off again to Katie Bannister's hotel. He felt tense. Wishing-he-didn't-have-to-do-this tense? Expectant tense? He couldn't tell. He only knew they hadn't got off to the best of starts and Katie Bannister was alone in Rome. He wanted her to relax. He wanted to relax.

No, he didn't, Rigo conceded as he shouldered open the door of the small, dingy hotel. Relaxing was the last thing on his mind. He didn't have anything half so worthy in mind for Katie Bannister. His hunting instincts had brought him here. He couldn't get her out of his head, the contra-dictions—the primness, weighed against the logo on a shopping bag from one of the sexiest lingerie stores in Rome. Her excuse that it belonged to Antonia was a lie. He'd driven Antonia home and unless his little sister had eaten the bag she certainly didn't have it with her. Since then his imagination had dressed Signorina Bannister in lace and silk—which, bearing in mind he'd only seen her in an ugly brown suit before, had been quite a startling revelation.

He approached the reception desk with his package and made his request.

'*Mi dispiace*, I'm sorry, Signor Ruggiero, but there is no reply from Signorina Bannister's room.' The man behind the desk shrugged as he replaced the telephone receiver.

He should have known he would be recognised. It couldn't be helped. 'Could Signorina Bannister be in your restaurant?' He stared across into an uninviting and markedly empty dining room.

'We have no reservations tonight, Signor Ruggiero.'

No surprise there. 'Her room number?'

The man barely paused a beat—something to do with the money he had just pressed into his hand, no doubt, before telling him, 'Room one hundred and ten, Signor Ruggiero.'

There was no answer when he knocked on the door. He used the house phone to ring the hotel kitchen and ask them to put Antonia's picnic in their cold room. Someone would be up right away to collect it, he was told. He waited until the porter arrived, and then he returned to room one hundred and ten. Where would Katie Bannister go this time of night?

He knocked and waited. He heard sounds from the room and knocked again.

She answered the door cautiously, leaving the security lever in place.

'How many times do I have to tell you I don't bite?'

'Rigo?' Her voice rose at least an octave when she gasped his name.

'Unless I have a double…' He leaned back against the wall. The corridor was narrow and they were agreeably close. Signorina Prim's sexy voice had done it again, he registered, enjoying the sensation.

'What do you want?' she whispered nervously through the gap.

Admittedly this wasn't the type of reception he had antici-pated, or was used to, but then Katie Bannister wasn't his usual type of date. 'We had a dinner engagement, if you remember?'

'I told you I'd be eating dinner in my room.'

And he had chosen to ignore that. 'You haven't eaten yet?' he said with surprise. 'It's nine o' clock.' As if anyone in Rome ate before nine.

'I didn't say I haven't eaten.' She opened the door a little wider and bit her lip.

She looked cute. 'You didn't say you have eaten,' he pointed out. 'Open the door, Katie. I can't stand here all night.'

The bar slid back and the door opened, but instead of standing to one side to let him in, she retreated into the shadows at the far end of the room.

CHAPTER SEVEN

'GOOD evening, Signorina Bannister. I trust I find you well?'

'Good evening, Rigo,' she said shyly, remaining pressed back against the wall.

'You look nice.' He closed the door softly behind him. Nice? She looked beautiful, which raised a number of questions. But taking things at face value to begin with, he knew her taste in lingerie and had already dallied with erotic images, but seeing this new, softer side had unexpectedly brought out the best in him. Until his suspicions raced to the fore. 'I beg your pardon for calling so late.'

She glanced at her wristwatch.

'And it seems you were going out?' After refusing his dinner invitation, was it possible the waiter won her over?

'I wasn't going anywhere.'

Was that a wistful note in her voice? 'But the dress?'

'I was just trying it on.' Raising her chin, she looked at him steadily. 'I bought it today. I don't know what I was thinking—'

'That it suited you?' he suggested.

'Do you really think so?'

In that moment she was like a child, and as pleasure flashed across her face she touched his heart, something that hadn't happened in a long time. 'Yes, I do. You look great.' Fragile, proud and womanly he didn't say. Even her profile with her hair scraped back so tightly was delicately appealing.

'I was going to return it—'

'Don't you dare—I mean, do as you like,' he said casually as she looked at him in surprise. She wasn't the only one to be surprised by the force of his reaction. 'So…you're not going out, but you'd like to?'

'Not really…' She made a little hand gesture. 'I'm fine right here—'

'But a dress like that is meant to be worn by a beautiful woman on a warm evening in Rome.'

She all but said, that rules me out.

'An evening just like this…'

She laughed nervously as he gestured towards the mean little window. 'It's very kind of you, Rigo—'

'I don't do kind. I'm hungry.'

'But you just ate with Antonia—'

'Fiddly food?' He dismissed the gourmet feast he'd enjoyed with an airy gesture. 'And, as you can see—' he ran a hand down his casual shirt and jeans '—I'm off-duty now.'

She risked a laugh.

'I'm thinking pizza—though Antonia sent a picnic for you, if you prefer?'

'I love your sister!' she exclaimed impulsively. 'Only Antonia would think of a picnic.'

He gave her a wry look. He couldn't deny Antonia held the record for delivering the unexpected, and doing it well. 'The hotel has it in their cold room—but I'm thinking real Roman pizza.'

He could see she was tempted.

'I'd have to get changed.'

'Into what?'

Her warning look told him not to make light of this because she hadn't made up her mind yet.

'You'd have to leave the room while I get changed.'

'I'm not going anywhere. And you're not getting changed. You're fine as you are. Here, grab this.' Snatching up a shawl from the bed, he tossed it to her.

She caught it.

'Now throw it round your shoulders and let's get out of here.'

He gave her no chance to change her mind. Opening the door, he ushered her through.

This wasn't a walk on the wild side—it was absolute lunacy. The moment they left the hotel she felt naked. She never went out in a flimsy summer dress. To do so with Rigo made her feel more vulnerable than ever.

And to think of all the things she could have done to get out of this—she could have played the tiredness card, the headache, the work to finish, the phone call to make, but instead she had fallen under Rigo's spell. It didn't help that he looked like a man from the pages of myth and legend. In casual clothes he was more aggressively virile than she had ever seen him and fitted perfectly into the template of ancient Rome. With his stern features and rugged, fighting form, he could have been a gladiator; the best.

As Rigo eased his pace to accommodate her shorter stride Katie wondered how safe her heart was. As he glanced at her with eyes like back-lit emerald that promised all the danger she could take, she concluded it was her chastity she should be concerned about. Could she trust herself to behave?

Did she want to behave?

If she was ever going to experience lovemaking, wouldn't it be better to do so under the tutelage of an expert?

'I'm not moving too fast for you, am I?'

Her cheeks flushed pink with guilty thoughts. 'Not at all…' *Not as fast as my fantasies would have you move.*

The dangerous smile creased his cheeks and fired every nerve in her body. She was transfixed by lips that curved in a firm and knowing smile. He knew how to walk close but not touching. He must know how that made her long to touch him—

And right on cue her scars shouted a stinging hello. They might be covered by the prettiest silk fabric, but they hadn't gone away and were as ugly as ever. And now the doubts crept in. What if Rigo put his arm round her shoulders? What if his hand strayed down her back? What if he pressed those long, lean fingers against her? He couldn't help but feel the ridges. And her final thought? What if he was repulsed by them?

Breathe deeply and stay calm, Katie's sensible self advised. Rigo hadn't made any attempt to touch her and was unlikely to do so. She might be dressed up by her own small-town standards, but she was hardly a femme fatale. This outing was merely a courtesy Signor Rigo Ruggiero was extending to a representative of the legal firm handling his brother's will.

To prove it, they were walking alongside each other like a couple of friends—

Friends?

Friends looked at each other's crotch, did they?

Katie wished her inner voice would shut up and stop acting as her conscience. Rigo's gaze might never stray, but she hadn't perfected the technique of not looking at something so prominently displayed.

What else was he supposed to do with it? her inner voice piped up again.

OK, so he was blessed in every department, but she didn't

have to fixate, did she? Hadn't she worked out yet how acute his senses were? Did she want him to know she had a crush?

They had reached a crossing and he stared down at her. 'Are you OK?'

'Perfectly.' But she flinched when he put his hand in the small of her back to steer her across the road.

'Relax.'

Yes, relax. What did she think? That he had X-ray vision now?

'You really are tense…'

She gasped as he caught hold of her hand and quickly concealed it in a cough. Was this supposed to help?

'What are you doing?' he said as she broke free. 'The traffic is dangerous and unpredictable—'

Like Rigo. 'Sorry—I promise to be more careful.'

'I'll make sure of it.' He locked his arm around her shoulder.

For a moment she didn't breathe. Surely he must feel her trembling? And then he walked her straight past the pizza place.

'That's for tourists,' he said as she turned her head.

She had to scurry along to keep up with his easy, loping stride. That wasn't easy on legs that felt like jelly. For the first time in her life she longed for her cheap suit. It might be ugly, but both the fabric and the shape were concealing. 'So where *are* we going?'

'First, we take a bus—'

'A bus?' He really was the master of surprises, she registered silently.

'Unless a tour bus isn't grand enough for you, Signorina Bannister?'

'It's fine by me.' And was what she had wanted to do all along. 'I'm just surprised you take buses…'

'You mean, a man like me?' he said. Rigo's face creased in a smile. 'I know every way there is to get around Rome.' He helped her onto the running board. 'I haven't always travelled by private jet.' He broke off to dig in the pocket of his jeans for some money to pay their fare.

A curtain lifted. She saw him clearly as the youth who had come to Rome with nothing and had made his fortune here. She only realised she was still frowning as she thought about it when Rigo dipped his head to stare her in the eyes. Her heart thundered a warning. 'It's only a bus trip costing a few euros,' he said. 'You can deduct it from your fee, if that makes you feel better?'

Better he misunderstood than read every thought in her head too clearly. 'I'm good—'

'Please allow me to reassure you that I have no intention of compromising your professional duties in any way, Signorina Bannister.'

He made her laugh. His humour was more dangerous than she knew.

And then the self-doubt crept in. Was that what he thought of her? She was all duty and no fun? That equalled dull in any language.

He chivvied her up the stairs. 'The view is better up here.'

He persuaded her to take a seat at the front. She checked her skirt was pulled down as she sat. No wonder Rigo thought her dull. He was easygoing, charming and, even in denim jeans and a fitted casual shirt clinging tenaciously to every hard-wired inch of his impressive torso, he was sex on two strong muscled legs. While she was—

'*Dolcezza.*'

'What?' He was paying her a compliment. Why couldn't she just accept it?

Maybe because, having sprawled across the seat next to her, Rigo was looking at her in a way that made her cheeks burn.

'I like the new look, Katie; keep it.'

Before she could reprimand him for using her first name he draped an arm around her shoulder and drew her close. 'Though I think you should be tempted to let your hair down.'

The murmured words sent her senses haywire as his warm breath connected with her ear. That must be why it took her a moment to realise what he meant to do, and by then it was too late. As he removed the single tortoiseshell pin from her hair it cascaded around her shoulders.

'*Bene,*' he said, sitting back.

'My hair ornament, please.' She held out her hand.

'You can have it back later,' he said, putting it in his pocket. 'Now concentrate on the view.'

As he spoke, what might well be his ancestral home hove into view. The Colosseum—the ancient amphitheatre with its pitted archways glowing eerily with honeyed light.

But as Rigo related the history of the building she was gripped. Discovering the man beneath the public face was a non-stop revelation. His depth aroused her to the point where it was no longer possible to concentrate. She had to shift position to ease the ache inside her. She wanted to remain immune to him and soon realised what a pointless exercise that was. What she really wanted was for Rigo to touch her intimately. All this she accepted whilst maintaining a serious conversation about ancient Rome.

CHAPTER EIGHT

EXPANDING her fantasies as the tour bus drove on into the night allowed for Rigo touching her skilfully and persistently, rhythmically and expertly, until she found release. It didn't stop there. They might experiment in the Colosseum—before a concert, maybe. As her gaze slipped to his lips while he talked she indulged in another image—one that stirred her more than most: she was being held down by Rigo while he subjected her to a lengthy feast of pleasure. She wanted sex with him. Which meant it was time to put a stop to such a dangerous fantasy.

Thankfully, Rigo provided the exit she had been looking for, when he thanked her for giving Antonia such a good day.

'It was my pleasure. Your sister is wonderful—and in fairness, it was Antonia who went out of her way to give me a good time.'

'Well, my little sister sees it another way. Come on, we get off here,' he said, standing up.

'But we're not back at the hotel.' She looked in vain for a landmark she recognised.

'Pizza?' Rigo reminded her.

But they seemed to be in the middle of nowhere. Katie frowned.

'I asked the bus driver to drop us here. Come on.' Rigo indicated that she must go ahead of him.

She disembarked onto a dimly lit street. Could this be right? Her skin prickled with apprehension.

'I don't have a clue where I am,' Rigo murmured.

But when she glanced at him in alarm, he smiled.

'You're teasing me—'

'Would I?'

She refused to hold that gaze, and stared instead at the bus as it drove away.

'I haven't always lived in the best part of Rome.'

She couldn't resist the hook and followed him.

'When I left my home in Tuscany and came to Rome I found myself in the Monti—all narrow lanes and steep inclines. It's where craftsmen ply their trade and there was always plenty of casual work for a strong boy from the country.'

By now she was consumed with curiosity. To learn about this other side of Rigo was irresistible.

'Is this our destination?' she said when he stopped walking on the high point of a bridge spanning the River Tiber. As she stared into Rigo's dazzlingly handsome face, waiting for his reply, she got another feeling—he enjoyed showing off his city to someone who wouldn't mock him for how poor he'd been. He still liked these offbeat trails to places that held no appeal for the fashionistas.

He was resting his hands on the stone balustrade, staring out across the river. Her heart picked up pace as he turned to look at her. Suddenly it didn't matter where they were going, and as crazy as it might seem they had reached at least one erotic destination, which was enough for her.

He broke the spell. 'Come on.' Straightening up, he reached for her hand and this time she didn't resist him. She even managed to persuade herself that it made perfect sense for Rigo to take her hand if they had to cross a busy main road. What did she know about Roman traffic? What did anyone know? Even the Romans didn't know. No one on earth could predict the unpredictable.

She shrank against him, glad of his protection as cars and scooters buzzed around them like angry bees. This contact with Rigo was the most foreplay she'd ever had. On that short journey to safety on the other side tiny darts of pleasure raced up her arm and spread…everywhere.

Rigo led her way up some stone steps that curved steeply around the outside of an ancient lookout tower. A pair of these towers marked either end of the bridge. 'This is the best place in Rome to watch the fireworks,' he explained, 'and it's free.'

She saw the boy he must have been—a boy who hadn't wasted time wailing about his fate, but who had squeezed the last drop of enjoyment out of his new life. And the way her heart swelled in admiration was a very worrying development indeed.

At the top of the tower she had to stop to catch her breath and, resting her arms on the warm stone, she leaned over the battlements.

'Since when can you fly?' Rigo demanded, pulling her back.

Having someone look out for her felt so good and as he stared down even breathing was difficult. He was close enough now for her to feel his body heat warming her.

She turned away. She wasn't sure how to deal with her feelings or this situation. She was going home tomorrow. They were complete opposites. This was one casual night in Rigo's life, but her life could be changed for good—

'Open your eyes, Katie, or you'll miss the fireworks.'

There was so much sensation dancing through her veins she barely registered the first fantastic plumes of sparkling colour. And then Rigo reached over her shoulder to point out some more, and as he did so he brushed her cheek. It made her turn and now their faces were only millimetres apart. She looked away, but not quickly enough. A darkly amused stare was her reward. He must know how strongly she was attracted to him. Did he also know how frustrated she was? Or what agony it was for her to be this close to him? Or that he made her body ache with need and longing?

He pulled back when the fireworks were over, allowing her to breathe freely again. She gulped in air enough to say, 'Thank you for bringing me here.'

'It isn't finished yet.' Spanning her waist with his hands, Rigo turned her to face the river.

There was no way to express her feelings towards what she could see, or what she could sense. Fireworks were falling from the sky, replacing the streamers of moonlight on the river with a dancing veil of fire. And there was fire in her heart.

Leaving the bridge, they walked deeper into the old part of the city. 'Ancient palaces!' Katie exclaimed with pleasure, staring about.

'Once this was a very grand area indeed,' Rigo confirmed, 'and now I have another surprise for you.' As he spoke he opened a street door and a blaze of light and heat burst out.

And good cooking smells, Katie registered, inhaling appreciatively as Rigo held the door open for her. He had brought her to a small, packed pizzeria where the noise of people enjoying themselves was all-enveloping.

'Don't worry,' he said, dipping his head to speak to her when he saw her hesitation, 'you'll be safe with me.'

He had also guessed correctly that she rarely went out, Katie thought wryly. She was glad of Rigo's encouragement.

There was a tiny dance floor on which a number of couples were entwined and a small group of musicians tucked away in a corner. Surrounding this, tables with bright red gingham cloths were lit by dripping candles rammed into old wine bottles.

'Do you like it?' Rigo shouted to her above the noise.

'I love it.' And she loved the feel of his arm around her shoulders.

The party atmosphere was infectious, but she was shy. Without Rigo she would never have ventured into a place like this. But when she took a proper look around and realised that all the other customers were as down-to-earth as she was, she relaxed. This certainly wasn't the type of nightlife she had imagined Rigo would indulge in. And she liked him all the better for it.

'Will you stop trying to tuck your hair behind your ears?' he said as they waited for a seat.

'I'm just not used to it hanging loose—'

'Then you should be. You have lovely hair. Leave it alone,' he insisted. 'You look fine. Ah—' he stepped forward as a portly man dressed in chefs trousers bustled over to them '—I'd like you to meet my friend Gino.'

Katie gathered Gino was the patron.

'Rigo! Brigante!' he exclaimed, clapping the much taller man on the back. 'Why is it I can't get rid of you?'

Katie suspected that both men knew the answer to that, judging from the warmth in their eyes as they stared at each other.

'And who is this?' Gino demanded, turning his shrewd, raisin-black stare Katie's way.

'This is Signorina Bannister…an associate of mine.'

'An associate?' Gino gave Katie an appreciative once-over before shaking hands with her. 'You must think a lot of your associate to bring Signorina Bannister to meet me?' He looked at Rigo questioningly, but Rigo's shrug admitted nothing.

'Signorina Bannister is in need of real Italian pizza before she leaves Rome. Where else would I take her, Gino?'

'Where else indeed?' Gino agreed. 'And for such a beautiful *signorina* I have reserved the best table in the house.'

'But you're full,' Katie observed worriedly. She didn't want to cause anyone any trouble. 'And how could you know we were coming?'

'I don't need to know,' Gino informed her, touching his finger to his nose. 'I keep my own special table ready at all times for my *speciale* guests…'

Before she could stop him Gino had whisked away her shawl. 'Oh, no!' Katie exclaimed, reaching for it, feeling suddenly naked again.

'You won't need a shawl here,' Gino assured her. 'It's always too hot in my restaurant—'

'But I…'

Feeling exposed and self-conscious beneath Rigo's amused gaze, Katie could only stand and watch helplessly as the burly restaurateur disappeared into the cloakroom with her prized piece of camouflage equipment.

'Don't worry,' Rigo soothed. 'Gino will keep your shawl safe.'

Rigo saw her comfortably settled and then took the seat opposite, while Katie sat demurely, taking stock of her fellow diners. Every other woman around them had stripped down to bare arms and shoulders.

But they all had flawless skin—

'Do you mind if I roll back my sleeves?' Rigo said, misinterpreting her look.

He was halfway through the process and hardly needed her

permission. 'Go ahead.' She tried very hard not to stare at his massively powerful forearms and concentrated instead on a formidable steel watch that could probably pinpoint their position in relation to the moon. One thing was sure—Gino was right: it was hot in here. Steaming.

'Ten o'clock.'

'I beg your pardon?' Katie swiftly refocused as Rigo spoke.

'I said it's ten o'clock. I noticed you looking at my watch.'

'I was—'

'Not because you want to go home, I hope?'

Gino saved her further embarrassment, bringing them the pizzas they had ordered. They were delicious. A thin, crispy crust baked just the way she liked it was loaded with succulent vegetables and slicked with chilli oil. Beneath that a yummy layer of zesty tomato sauce was crowned with fat globs of melted cheese. She only realised how hungry she was when she took her first bite—and there was no polite way to eat pizza when you were this hungry.

'Now you see why Gino and I became such good friends,' Rigo said, leaning forward to mop her chin. 'There was always something he needed doing—and I always needed feeding after a hard day of manual labour.'

She could understand how their friendship had been forged. 'You found a mutual need,' she said. And could have bitten off her tongue as Rigo's gaze lingered. 'Indeed,' he agreed, sitting back. 'Napkin?' he suggested.

'Good idea…' Drool was not a good look. She returned her attention determinedly to her food.

'This is only the first course, to whet your appetite.'

'Oh, no. I really couldn't eat another thing…'

'If you lived in Italy you would soon develop a healthy appetite.'

She had no doubt. But was that wise?

Katie sensibly avoided Rigo's gaze, reminding herself she was going home tomorrow.

So? Didn't that mean she should make the most of today?

There was such a festival air in the small bistro Katie was soon tapping her foot in time to the music. Gino had insisted she must try his home-made wine—how right he was. Picking up her glass, she drank the delicious ruby-red liquid down. It was so moreish. Who needed brand names when the house wine tasted like this? She immediately craved more and held out her glass for a refill. 'It tastes just like cranberry juice—'

'And packs a kick like a mule,' Rigo warned. 'So drink it slowly…'

He really did think of her as a kid sister—that, or an ancient aunt. Of course she would drink it slowly.

Well, she had meant to, but it tasted so fruity and innocent, and one more glass couldn't hurt her surely?

'And now you must dance,' Gino insisted, waltzing past with an armful of plates.

'I don't dance.' She announced this to Rigo, who didn't seem to care whether she danced or not.

'Do what you like,' he said, leaning back in his chair.

It seemed to Katie that the young women at the pizzeria had no inhibitions at all, and that their sole reason for being here was to shimmy into Rigo's eye line. Something tight curled in her stomach as she watched them flash lascivious glances at him.

'Well, *signorina*,' Gino said on his return, 'will you make an old man happy?'

It took longer than Katie had expected to focus her eyes on Gino's face, and even longer to register surprise that he was serious. Gino did want to dance with her. Suddenly Rigo's warning about the wine made sense. Her head was on straight, but the room was tilting—and now Gino was opening his arms to her.

'Go ahead,' Rigo said helpfully as the band launched into a wild tarantella.

Having stumbled to her feet, she barely had chance to exclaim, as Gino, quite literally, whisked her off her feet.

CHAPTER NINE

RIGO cut in.

By the time he cut in Katie was happy to forget her reservations and fall into his arms.

Gino melted away.

Had she been set up? Katie wondered. A bleary glance into Rigo's totally sober face told her precisely nothing—at least, not in her present state. This was great. She couldn't dance. She could barely stand up. And Signor Superior had been proven right. The wine had gone to her head. And now she was in danger of making a complete fool of herself.

There was nothing for it, Katie concluded. Before she fell over she had to appeal to Rigo's better nature—that was, supposing he had one. 'If you could just get me back to our table…' When cast adrift in a storm of flying heels and elbows, it didn't do to stand on your pride.

But Rigo didn't lead her off the dance floor. Couldn't he understand? Hadn't he heard her? 'I don't dance,' she complained.

She got a reaction this time. One inky brow rose in elegant disbelief but, rather than leading her to safety, he tightened his grip on her arms. 'Everyone can dance, Signorina Bannister.'

'I absolutely don't dance.' And, taking that as her cue, she broke free and attempted to totter back to their table unaided.

Thankfully, Rigo caught her in his arms just as she was on the point of lurching into a waiter. 'I'm fine.' She flapped her arms around to demonstrate this.

'Well, clearly, you're not.' So saying, he banded her arms firmly to her body.

'Let me go.' Her breath caught in her throat as she stared into Rigo's amused gaze. 'I did warn you about the wine,' he pointed out, keeping a firm hold of her.

Right now the wine was the least of her worries.

And then at Rigo's signal the music changed abruptly. From jigging up and down like frantic monkeys the couples all around them eased effortlessly into the sinuous rhythm of the rumba.

'What did I tell you?' he soothed, murmuring in her ear. 'You dance beautifully…'

How could she not when Rigo had somehow managed to mould her clumsy body to his? And Rigo could dance.

Oh, yes, he could…

By some miracle she stopped wobbling, and began to move her feet in some sort of recognisable pattern. As long as he didn't hold her too close she'd be all right. As long as his hands didn't wander to the scars on her back she could do this.

And now she was even beginning to relax, it felt so safe and good…

Not so her fantasies. They weren't safe at all. Dancing close to Rigo with all the other couples masking them gave Katie's imagination all the excuse it needed. She had everything to learn about a man's body and this was her opportunity.

As the music filled her, her senses grew ever more acute. Her body was like molten honey curling round him until Rigo changed position and her fantasies flew away.

'What's wrong?' he said as she grew tense.

'Nothing...' She took a deep breath and tried to relax, but the magic had vanished. Rigo's hand had slipped into the hollow in the small of her back as they danced and then his fingers had eased a little higher. Good manners for him not to touch her anywhere remotely intimate, but a danger signal for her, and her head had cleared at once. There was no possibility she could relax now. Even her deepest longings stood no chance against her greatest fear. She wanted Rigo to hold her—she also wanted to be perfect. She wanted to rest unresisting in his arms, and dance and dream, and enjoy herself, but how could she with her scars?

'Katie?' Dipping his head, Rigo stared into her troubled eyes. 'If you concentrate on dancing the rest will follow.'

He couldn't know how wrong he was. But as he drew her to him there was something reassuring about him. The power of his command and the fact that she didn't want to make a scene...

His hands slipped lower. Theoretically she should be hearing more warning signals—and this time they wouldn't be connected with her scars, but her body was clamouring and she didn't want to fight it. This was like skirting the fringes of a hurricane and, instead of running as fast as she should in the opposite direction, hoping to be swept away by it.

'Let go,' Rigo murmured, encouraging her to relax.

But the damage was done and now she could think of nothing but securing her mate in the most primitive way possible. 'I'm trying to.'

If only she dared.

He was enjoying this far more than he had expected. His initial impulse had been to rescue Katie from the risk of being trampled by Gino's enthusiasm, but that was before he discovered how she felt beneath his hands. Timid, yet eager, she had everything to learn, and that in itself was irresistible.

He had to remind himself that she was going home tomorrow and there was no time for the style of initiation he had in mind. Resting his chin on her hair, he smiled as he dragged in her light, wild-flower scent. It was a revelation to him to feel how Katie trembled beneath his intentionally light touch. He knew she wanted more. She proved it by moving closer, seeking contact, seeking pressure between their bodies, seeking sex.

So was Signorina Prim strait-laced and just a little drunk, or was she a dam waiting to burst? Perhaps Katie Bannister was the best actress he had ever met. She was certainly a storm loosely contained in a cage of inexperience. He knew that he should take her back to the table and call for the bill, prior to taking her back to sleep alone in her chaste, maidenly bed.

And he would…soon.

If Rigo's hands should slip lower…

Katie gulped. She was relieved that he was nowhere near her scars, of course, but he was almost cupping her bottom, which had set off a chain reaction in parts of her she mustn't know about. But how could she hide her response to him? She didn't have the experience to know. She arched her back. She couldn't help herself. She wanted to feel those big, strong hands holding her. She wanted to read all the subliminal messages that could pass between a man and a woman through the merest adjustment of a finger…

As the sultry beat of the slow, Latin American dance thrilled through her Katie found herself angling her buttocks ever more towards Rigo's controlling hands. It was a signal as old as time and one he couldn't help but read.

She exhaled raggedly as he confirmed this by adjusting the position of his hands once again. His fingertips were dangerously close now and, rather than feeling alarm, she felt small and safe, and violently aroused. She had never done anything as bold as this before, but here in the wholesome surroundings of the simple pizzeria, hidden in a mass of dancing couples, she felt free from the usual constraints. Gazing up, she met with eyes as dark and watchful as the night. Lower still she saw the sardonic smile playing around the corners of Rigo's mouth, and realised he knew.

He knew.

She closed her eyes and tried to steady her breathing, when what she really wanted to do was whisper, make love to me. But, other than in her wildest and most erotic fantasy, she would never find the courage to do that.

His senses were on fire. For the first time in his life he didn't want a dance to end. The sexual chemistry between them had surprised him. He had enjoyed teasing Katie Bannister, the girl he thought of as Signorina Prim, but now his thoughts were taking the direct route to seduction. He wasn't alone in feeling the power of this erotic spell. The other couples on the dance floor were drawn to them like moths to immolate on erotic flame. Even the musicians were swept up in this inferno of desire and, with a key change like a sigh, had reinforced the mood.

But he didn't do one-night stands, or complications. Usually.

'You're quite a surprise to me,' he murmured, feeling her tremble as his breath brushed her ear.

'I wasn't always so dull…'

He wasn't going to argue about Katie's interpretation of dull. Sensing there was more to come, he remained silent.

'I trained to be an opera singer once.'

'Did you?' He couldn't have been more surprised and pulled back to stare into her eyes. 'What went wrong?'

He knew at once he shouldn't have asked. He hadn't meant to spoil the evening for her. Drawing her back into his arms, he held her gently and securely until she relaxed.

She'd tell him if she wanted to tell him, he reasoned. But the revelation had intrigued him. There was obviously so much more to uncover in this woman who favoured dull brown suits—perhaps an artistic diva waiting to break out. But as far as he was concerned, she must remain a shy, brown mouse who was under his protection while she was in Rome. Katie Bannister might be many things, but she was not a seductress—and even if in this sultry setting she appeared to be, it was up to him to keep things light between them and send her home as innocent as the day she had arrived in Italy.' Reluctantly he disentangled himself from her arms. '*Andiamo, piccolo topo—*'

'I am not your little mouse,' she slurred.

And then he realised that three glasses of wine was probably her annual quota back home and she had drunk Gino's firewater as if it were cordial—which almost certainly accounted for her openness about her opera training too.

'You must learn to call me Signorina Bannister,' she insisted, drawing her taupe brows together in her approximation of a fierce stare.

'*Bene,*' he said, happy to indulge her—at least on that one point.

'It's much better if we keep it…' She frowned as she searched for the right word.

'Formal between us?' he suggested. 'I think it's time I took you home now,' he said firmly, holding her away from him at arm's length.

Rigo's sudden change of mood from sexy to serious was so unexpected Katie blanked for a moment. Only when she finally managed to refocus did she wonder how she had ever wasted a moment thinking Rigo Ruggiero uncomplicated and fun. He was a playboy who lived every moment for the pleasure it brought him before moving on to the next distraction. Gino's genuine warmth and the restaurateur's homely restaurant must have clouded her thinking.

OK, that and the wine.

Common sense should have warned her Rigo was not the youth who had pitched up in Rome hoping to make his fortune. Rigo enjoyed these nostalgic visits but that didn't mean he was the same uncomplicated youth he'd been then.

As he frogmarched her back to the table she faced the ugly truth. She was as naïve as she had ever been and Rigo was the same playboy for whom the main attraction on tonight's menu of amusement had been an impressionable out-of-towner. He'd played the game for a while, but had soon tired of her lack of sophistication. She felt bad, because she never put herself in the way of rejection, knowing the outcome was a foregone conclusion. And the one time she had...

Katie smiled as she thanked Gino for her shawl. Rigo was already standing by the door, waiting for her. He couldn't wait to bring the evening to a close. It was up to her to pull herself together and leave with enough pride to be able to deal with him on a professional level tomorrow morning.

Taking a shower in cold reality was the swiftest antidote to male pride he knew. As he held the restaurant door for Katie her cool gaze assured him—don't worry, you won't get the chance. Tipping her chin, she walked proudly past him into the night. Even that amused him. Most women with one eye on his fortune tried harder. Katie wasn't that sort. In her eyes he was a man who preferred racing his sports car to keeping an appointment. Shallow? He was barely puddle-deep. Yes, all this he could see in Katie Bannister's cool, topaz-coloured gaze.

He only had to raise his hand and a limousine drew up in front of them at the kerb. 'Your chariot awaits, *signorina*. I plan ahead,' he said when she looked at him in surprise. 'Don't worry,' he added when her gaze flickered with alarm. 'I'll see you safely back to your hotel.'

He let his driver help her into the car, which appeared to reassure her. He took his seat in the back, ensuring he kept a good space between them. She didn't risk further conversation; neither did he. It seemed the most sensible course of action after the fire they'd ignited at Gino's. He glanced at his wristwatch and was surprised by the way time had flown. 'If you'd like to make our meeting a little later—'

'Not at all,' she interrupted in a way that drew his attention to her lips. She had beautifully formed plump pink lips. The thought of pressing his mouth against them while his tongue teased them apart stirred him. He could imagine how she would taste, and how it would feel when she wound her arms around his neck. 'In that case, I suggest we have lunch immediately afterwards—'

'Immediately after our meeting tomorrow I'll be on a plane home, Signor Ruggiero.'

He awarded her more than one brownie point for that swift riposte. 'I thought we'd agreed you'd call me Rigo?'

She didn't answer, and as she turned away to stare out of the window he found the chill between them erotic. He liked a challenge. And, even if he had decided to take her home and treat her chastity with the respect it deserved, he was a man.

She spoiled the mood by asking for her hair clip.

He shrugged and gave it to her, and then had to watch as she scraped her hair back as tightly and as primly as it would go. She only relaxed when she had completed the transformation from lovely young woman to maiden aunt.

But the obvious had always bored him, which was why Katie Bannister intrigued him. So much passion so tightly controlled could only end one way. And remembering her visit to his favourite shop—what a contrast that style of underwear would be to her precisely ordered hair. When did she intend on wearing it? Was she wearing it? What had provoked Signorina Prim into that walk on the wild side? And what would persuade her to take another walk on the wild side with him?

As if sensing the path his thoughts were taking, she looked at him shyly, but, shy or not, that look plainly said he shouldn't imagine everything had been put on this earth for his amusement.

'In another thirty-six hours,' she said, and with rather too much relish, he thought, 'I'll be back at my desk in Yorkshire—'

'In that case we'll have to work quickly,' he said.

She flashed him a concerned glance.

'I'll take you to the airport immediately after the reading of the will.'

He felt sure she would refuse this offer, but instead she said, 'Thank you, Signor Ruggiero, that will save me taking a cab.'

Katie was on tenterhooks until they reached the hotel. She couldn't wait to bury her head under a pillow and wish the night away so it could be morning and she could gabble out the contents of the will and go home to her dull, quiet, *safe* life. To her disappointment, for the remainder of the journey home Rigo had no trouble keeping things on a business footing and didn't speak to her at all. By the time they reached the hotel she was tied up in knots.

He escorted her across the lobby and even insisted on

pressing the elevator button. When the lift doors slid open he kept his finger on that button as he said, 'Goodnight, Signorina Bannister. I hope you sleep well. And don't worry about calling a cab in the morning—I will send a car for you.'

She said thank you for the evening and then got into the lift. She wished, hoped, prayed, Rigo would step in after her. Of course, he didn't. Something she had every cause to be grateful for, Katie reasoned sensibly as the elevator door closed.

After that everything felt flat and a restless night followed. There was only one face in her dreams, which explained why her eyes were red the next morning. Her face was washed-out too, and as for her hair…

Better not to dwell on that disaster, she decided, scraping it back neatly into the customary bun before securing the severe style with the whole of a packet of hair grips.

Job done, she stared at her reflection in the mirror. Unfortunately, the image hadn't changed. She was the same ordinary person. The next task was automatic. Angling her head to stare at her naked back in the mirror, she checked her scars. Nothing had changed there either. They were still as livid, the sight of them just as stomach-churning.

What had she expected? Did she think she could wish them away?

Impatient with herself for this moment of weakness, she turned away to dress in modest brown. There was only one thing out of sync in this neat brown package, she concluded after slipping on her sensible brown court shoes, and that was some rather striking underwear, purchased from a luxury boutique in Rome. Well, if she waited for a suitable opportunity to wear it the moths would have a feast.

Before leaving the room she slicked on some lip gloss. Mashing her lips together experimentally, she decided to wipe it off again. Did she want to draw attention? As no other delaying tactics sprang to mind, she drew in a deep, steadying breath and picked up her bag.

CHAPTER TEN

HE SETTLED his shades in place. Zapping the lock, he swung into the car. Resting the phone in its nest, he was still talking, grim-faced and tight-lipped as he pulled away from the kerb outside the imposing hospital building. 'Yes, of course, do everything you can—whatever it takes—and please keep me informed.'

He stopped and drew breath as he cut the line. Now it was business as usual. This was his life—swinging from the charity that meant so much to him to the business that sustained it. The only difference today was that he was going to be late again for a meeting with Katie Bannister.

It couldn't be helped and he wouldn't explain the delay. He didn't want the world knowing what he did in his private time and only a very few individuals knew he was behind the charitable foundation. His only concern was ensuring confidentiality for anyone helped by the foundation. Today it had provided life-saving surgery; tomorrow he might be taking a teenager around the track in his sports car. Whatever was required he made time for—and sometimes Antonia suffered; he knew that and felt bad about it, but there were never enough hours in a day.

Antonia knew nothing about this other life. She was too

young. He would never put the burden of silence on her shoulders.

Resting his unshaven chin on his arm, he waited for a gap in the traffic. Before he could placate Antonia he must meet with Signorina Prim, and learn what last thought Carlo had sent his way. Katie Bannister would be cooling her sensible heels at the penthouse, feeling justly affronted because he was late by more than an hour.

In spite of the rush-hour traffic he made it back in record time. Leaving the sports car where it was sure to be clamped and in all probability towed away, he raced into the building. He stabbed impatiently at the elevator button and barged inside the steel cage before the doors were properly open. Throwing himself back against the wall, he watched the floor numbers changing—more slowly, surely, than they had ever changed before.

Edgy didn't even begin to describe his condition. Impatience steaming out of every pore. He used the few seconds remaining to compartmentalise his thinking. He couldn't take so much anger and concern into this meeting—it wasn't fair to Katie. She didn't know about his day, or the fact that Carlo was trying to stab him one last time from the grave—how could she?

He liked her. She was a quiet little mouse, but the way she stood up to him suggested there was a spine of steel in there somewhere—who wouldn't like that? Maybe if things had been different…

But things weren't different and the elevator had just reached his floor.

She found it hard to believe Rigo would be late again. Surely, not even he could be this inconsiderate—this rude? It proved how little he thought of her professionally; in every way. She was an inconvenience and nothing more. Staring down at the busy main road framed by exquisite palaces and gardens, Katie tried to make herself believe it didn't matter Rigo was late again. Why should she care? This was business. Lots of clients were late for business meetings—some even forgot about them entirely. Why should this be any different?

Because this appointment was with Rigo.

Because of the ache in her heart.

Because she wanted him to treat her better than the average client would treat her, and because she had allowed herself to commit the cardinal sin of becoming emotionally involved with a client—a one-sided arrangement that left her feeling daft and stupid. As she continued to beat herself up her attention was drawn to one of the large Roman car-towing vehicles. No doubt someone else's day was about to be spoiled—

'Katie.'

She whirled around as Rigo's husky voice broke the silence.

'I'm so sorry.' He strode towards her. Having burst in like a whirlwind, he spread his arms wide in a gesture of regret. 'Please accept my apologies.'

She took him in at a glance—the unshaven face, the rumpled clothes, the less than brilliant eyes. A horrible thought occurred to her, making her feel sick inside. Had he come here straight from someone's bed?

And why should she care? Was his sex life her business now?

But she did care. She cared a great deal too much. 'Rigo,' she said, extending a cool hand in greeting. 'I had almost given you up.'

'You've been well looked after, I hope?' He glanced around and relaxed when he saw her coffee.

'I've been looked after very well, thank you, and while I was waiting—'

'Yes?'

His eyes were warmer now. 'I took down some messages for you.'

'*Bene*…good.'

She crossed to the desk to pick up the notes she had made. 'One was from the PA you just sacked,' she said, turning. 'Signorina Partilora was most disappointed that you weren't here for her to deliver her message to you in person. Perhaps you'd like me to read it to you—'

'No,' he interrupted. 'That's OK. I can imagine…'

'If you're sure?' Her eyes glinted.

'Signorina Bannister,' Rigo growled, 'if I am any judge, I cannot imagine that such words would ever cross your lips.'

Then I might surprise you, Katie thought, flashing her innocent look. 'I think it's safe to say Signorina Partilora will not be working for you again,' she told him mildly.

Rigo laughed. 'What a relief. I have your cast-iron guarantee on that, do I?'

He was close enough to touch and her senses were ignited by his delicious man scent. If she could bottle that warm, clean, spicy aroma she'd make a fortune, Katie concluded. And then she would be able to walk away from a job she had no passion for.

'The will?' Rigo prompted.

'Yes, of course.' Her eyes stung with tears as she walked to the desk.

Because this was the end, Katie realised. It was the end of her Roman fantasy and the end of her fantasy life with Rigo—except she had no life with Rigo and she'd be going home after this.

Instead of sitting across from her Rigo came up behind her and put his hands on her shoulders. His touch was electric. Had he seen her eyes fill with tears? She couldn't bear the humiliation.

'I understand why you are upset and short tempered,' he said, keeping his hands in place, 'and you have every right to be angry with me. Please be assured my delay was necessary.'

She let her breath out slowly as he lifted his hands away and walked to the other side of the desk. She found it even harder to control her feelings when Rigo was nice to her, and now her nose was having a seizure, while her throat felt as if someone was standing on it. 'Shall we start?' she managed hoarsely.

'Of course,' he said.

She focused her attention on the legal documents in front of her, but the imprint of Rigo's fingers on her shoulders remained. She had to remind herself Rigo was Italian and caresses came easily to him. Such shows of emotion were practically unheard of in Katie's world—except perhaps under the office mistletoe at Christmas, when the ancient caretaker made sure she wasn't left out and always gave her a peck on the cheek.

Rigo made a sign for her to begin.

Must he sprawl across the seat? Must he look quite so sexy even in repose?

In the best acting scene of her life, she began.

Grim-faced, he listened. Carlo had left him everything? His mouth curved with distaste. He couldn't wait to find out what 'everything' entailed. He guessed debt would play some part in it. Katie caught sight of his expression and gave him a troubled glance.

Getting up from the desk, he turned his back on her. Today he could have used her soothing presence and common sense. Today he wanted nothing more than to have this sordid business over with so he could ring the hospital. *If they didn't ring him first...*

'There's also a private letter from your stepbrother, Rigo, as well as a small package.'

Katie's soft voice cut through his thoughts and he heard her push back her chair, get up and walk across the room towards him.

'*Grazie.*' He turned.

'I'll leave you, shall I?' she offered, hovering uncertainly.

'No.' He held out his hand, palm up. 'Stay. Please,' he added, when her steady gaze called him to account for his brusque manner.

He walked some distance away before opening Carlo's letter. Katie could have no idea of the depths of depravity to which his stepbrother had sunk and the disgrace Carlo had brought on the family. He didn't want her to know. Why give her that as a parting gift to take home? Like his visit to the hospital earlier, none of this was Katie's responsibility. Let her return to England with her presumptions about his glittering life intact. Just so long as she left Rome as carefree as she arrived he was fine with that.

After years of practice he thought he was immune to feeling, but the sight of Carlo's familiar hand gave him a punch in the gut he hadn't expected. He glanced at Katie, who discreetly looked away. He had shut himself off emotionally years back when his father had chosen a woman and that woman's son over him. The same loneliness and isolation he'd felt then swept over him now.

He tensed, hearing Katie ask him softly, 'Are you all right?'

He nodded curtly and turned back to Carlo's letter. His heart was closed.

Wasn't it?

Dragging the usual mental armour round him, he began to read.

Rigo—
There is nothing I can say to make up for the years I
stole from you, but I want to make my peace with you
before I die. I'm not giving you anything that isn't right-
fully yours.
Carlo.

Cryptic to the end, he thought, ripping open the small
package.

The keys of the family *palazzo* in Tuscany tumbled into
his hands, followed by his father's ring. He slipped on the ring
and felt both the weight of responsibility it carried and an
agonising longing. He had waited so long for contact with his
father, and that it should come like this…

And to see his home again…his beautiful home…

He lowered the letter to his side as a well of emotion
threatened to drown him.

The here and now fell away as his mind travelled back to
the past. He had lived a blissful country existence at the
palazzo, ignorant of pomp and pretension until his father fell
in love and brought Carlo and his stepmother home. He had
welcomed Carlo with open arms, thinking he would have a
brother to share things with, only to have his youthful naïvety
thrown back in his face. Carlo hadn't had time to spare for a
boy much younger than him, and one who stood in the way of
easy money.

'Shall I get you a drink?'

He glanced up, still a little disorientated as Katie spoke to
him. 'No. Yes…a glass of water…please.'

'I'll go and get it for you.'

Her expression told him she understood something of what
he was going through, and for the briefest of moments there
was a real connection between them.

Everything had come full circle, he realised as Katie left him to pace. She was going home. He was going home. He could hardly take it in. He would have liked a bit longer to get used to the idea, but there was no time.

Katie returned a little later with a tray of coffee, hot and strong. She brought him some iced water too. He guessed she had wanted to leave him alone with his thoughts for a while.

'That's very good of you, Signorina Bannister,' he said as she laid everything out for him, 'but I should take you to the airport now.' He glanced at his watch, feeling his head must explode from everything he'd learned.

'There's time enough for that.' She busied herself making sure his coffee was poured the way he liked it.

'I thought you were in a hurry to get back to England.'

'I can't leave you like this—'

'Like what?' he demanded sharply. He didn't need her pity. What business was it of hers how he felt?

She raised her steady gaze to his and as if a veil had lifted a torrent of impassioned words poured out. 'I do this all the time, Rigo—I see this all the time. I can't stand it. I can't stand how cruel people can be to each other.'

'Then you should toughen up.'

'Or get out of the job,' she said thoughtfully.

'There is that,' he agreed, watching her as he sipped the hot, aromatic liquid.

She calmed him. Against all the odds, Katie Bannister calmed him. Dread at what the contents of the will might reveal had been replaced by shock when he'd learned that Carlo had left him the only place he cared about. The *palazzo* had been in the Ruggiero family for centuries and Carlo must have recognised this at the end, so there was some good in him after all. The question now was, could he live with the guilt of knowing the past could never be mended?

Turning away from Katie, he passed a hand over his eyes. Too much emotion.

But he was going home…

Home…

Growing elation was threatening to leave him on the biggest high he'd ever known. He wanted someone to share that feeling with. He wanted Katie to share it with him, but she was already packing up her things, a little hesitantly, he thought. 'What's on your mind?' She looked as if she was struggling with a decision.

'Oh…you know…' She flapped her hand, dismissing his concern.

'No, I don't know. I want you to tell me. What's wrong?' He was feeling increasing concern for this quiet girl who made everyone else's problems her own and yet seemed so isolated, somehow.

'You have your own problems.'

As always she made light of her own concerns. 'I just inherited an estate and a *palazzo* in Tuscany,' he pointed out. 'How bad can it be?'

'That must mean a lot to you.' All her focus was on him now.

'My birthright? Oh, you know…' He dismissed the home of his dreams, his childhood and his heart with an airy gesture.

'Don't, Rigo. You make it sound so flippant, when anyone with half an ounce of sense can see how much this means to you.'

'You can tell, maybe…' It was a turning point. He wanted the moment to last, but the best thing for Katie was for him to let his driver take her to the airport. A more unworthy part of him was reacting in the age-old way in the face of death. He wanted sex. The urge to make new life was an imperative inborn command. He wanted to have sex with Katie Bannister.

CHAPTER ELEVEN

WHAT was wrong with him? After years of emotional abstinence, why this sudden roller-coaster ride? He'd had huge and fantastic coups in business many times and hadn't felt a thing. He'd learned long ago to turn his back on an inheritance he thought he'd never see again. So it wasn't the just the *palazzo* in Tuscany gnawing at his gut. Was it possible this shy, innocent girl was slowly melting his resolve and bringing emotion into his life?

He watched Katie cross the room to the desk in her neat, precise way. Her feelings were bound up tight just like his. He would like to see her respond to life and all its opportunities, and with abandon.

'Before I go, here is the list of phone messages I took for you,' she said in her strait-laced way. 'And don't be offended, but while I was waiting for you I tidied up that pile of documents by your chair on the floor—'

'I meant to get round to that.'

'How many PAs have you sacked?' she asked him bluntly.

Many, but did he want to frighten her off with an idea being born in his head? 'I'm not the easiest man to work for,' he admitted with monumental understatement. 'I need someone who can use their initiative and do more than answer the phone—'

'Well, lucky for you,' she cut in dryly, 'I made a list of all the written messages I found lying around.'

'Most of them written on the back of envelopes,' he said, remembering his latest PA's failure to grasp the simple fact that a desk diary could be quite a useful office tool if she remembered to use it.

'Your diary is in quite a mess,' Katie added, levelling a stare on him.

'And has been for some time,' he agreed.

'And the staff at your office…'

Could be called obnoxious; he'd admit that. 'Go on,' he prompted, feeling there was something more to come.

'Have no manners at all,' she told him frankly. 'And that's not good for your image.'

'What image?'

'Exactly.'

He missed a beat. 'Why, Signorina Bannister, I think you just revealed another side to your character.'

'Really?'

'PA—'

'Oh, no.' Shaking her head, she laughed at the thought of him offering her a job.

'Pain in the ass?'

She stared at him and then laughed again. 'For a moment there I thought you were offering me a job—'

'Do you think I'm mad?' he teased her, watching closely for a reaction. Then he told himself the idea of employing her was mad; a momentary lapse of judgement. Did he want a woman who cared so much around him?

His phone rang, bringing these thoughts to an end.

He had a brief conversation before cutting the line.

He swung around, elated. 'Now I could kiss you—'

'Let's not get carried away,' she said awkwardly, losing no

time putting the desk between them. 'I don't like to rush you, but my flight leaves at four o' clock. You've had good news, I take it?'

'The best—'

It must have been one heck of a deal, Katie concluded. 'Congratulations—'

'Congratulate the doctors, not me—'

'The doctors?'

'A friend of mine has had an operation,' Rigo told her vaguely, ruffling his thick black hair. His glance was evasive and he gave her the impression that he thought he'd said too much already.

'I hope your friend's okay?'

'The operation went really well, apparently.'

'Then that's the best news you could have.'

'And it frees me to go to Tuscany right away.'

'Don't let me keep you. I can take a cab—'

'I wouldn't hear of it. I'll arrange a driver—'

And that would be the end of everything.

Katie froze as Rigo continued chatting about flight schedules. He'd been equally matter-of-fact when they had returned from their amazing evening together, when she'd felt anything but matter-of-fact. She'd been frightened by the strength of her feelings for him—out of her depth and bewildered that feelings could be so one-sided. She had longed to return to her safe, quiet life in Yorkshire, but now the opportunity to do so had arrived she didn't want the adventure to end. She wanted to stay until she knew the secret of Carlo's will, because something told her the contents would hurt Rigo. She had to be there for him, because she cared for him, she cared for him desperately.

There was an alternative, Katie's inner voice suggested— if she was brave enough.

'I could go back now,' she blurted, clumsily interrupting him, 'or…'

'Or?' Rigo echoed.

Would her mind re-engage in time to speak with clarity, when all this man had to do to melt every bone in her body was to turn and give her that look? 'Or I could come with you…' By now she was hyperventilating to the point where she thought she might faint.

'Come with me? I thought you couldn't wait to leave Rome?'

She would have to share at least part of her reason for wanting this, Katie realised. 'Can I tell you the truth?'

'I would expect nothing less of a lawyer,' Rigo responded dryly.

'I'm not even sure I'll have a job when I get home. You see, my firm's cutting back—'

'A failing firm doesn't mean you can't get a job elsewhere.'

'I'd take my chances,' she agreed, 'but I'm not sure I even want to be a lawyer.'

Rigo's brows shot up.

'I get too involved,' she explained. 'Everyone has to constantly remind me I'm not a social worker and should concentrate on the facts—'

'But you still care.'

'Yes, I do.'

'Is that something to be ashamed of?'

'No, but it might mean I'm in the wrong job.'

He laughed. It was a short, very masculine sound. 'And you think you'd be happier working for me? I don't think so, Signorina Bannister.'

'Oh, well…' Raising her arms a little, she dropped them to her sides. Of course Rigo didn't want her working for him.

He wanted someone slick and polished at his side. But a longing inside her stirred—a longing so strong she couldn't ignore it. This might be her one chance to embrace change and adventure and, yes, see him sometimes. She drew a deep breath. 'You can't keep a PA—'

'That's true.'

'I might not have the makings of a good lawyer, but I am incredibly organized.'

'And you care too much about people—'

'Not you,' she quickly assured him.

Pressing his hand against his chest, he gave her a mock-serious look. 'Of course not.'

'How about you take me on for a trial period?'

'Are you serious?'

'Absolutely.' She held his gaze. 'Your stepbrother has left you the family estate in Tuscany, but you haven't been there since you were a boy and you don't know what to expect when you get there. I could come with you and take notes— make suggestions. I have a passion for historical design— only a hobby,' she added quickly, cheeks flushing, knowing she was the last person on earth Rigo would turn to for advice. 'And I speak fluent Italian.' Her trump card.

'OK, OK,' he said, halting the flow of her enthusiasm with raised hands. 'Let's stop this fantasy right now. Do you have any idea what the drop-out rate is for my staff?'

'No, but I can imagine. Maybe you need an office manager too.'

'Are you creating a role for yourself, Signorina Bannister?'

'No, I'm identifying a need,' Katie argued. 'A mutual need.' She bit her lip as she came to the crux of it all. 'I need a change and you need a second string.'

'A second string?' Rigo's face creased in his trademark smile, but his eyes were steadily assessing her. 'Do you really think you can walk in here and, after five minutes' exposure to my world, be ready to work alongside me and understand my business? I don't think so—'

'No, of course I don't think that, but we'd both be new to this project—'

'Tuscany is not a project,' Rigo cut across her. 'The Palazzo Farnese is the past and, though I loved it once, I intend to sell it on. There are too many unhappy memories—'

'Good ones too—'

'Leave it,' he warned. 'You don't know me that well.'

Katie braced herself. 'But you are going to see it before you sell it on?'

'I said so, didn't I?'

'That's good.' She believed it was crucial he did. She'd seen the mixture of emotions pass behind Rigo's eyes when he realised Carlo had left him the *palazzo*—elation being one of them. 'Remedial work might be necessary before the *palazzo* goes on the market. You should make time—'

'Oh, should I?' His gaze turned cold. 'You're an expert, suddenly?'

No, but she knew one thing—Rigo mustn't treat this bequest like a cold-blooded business deal or he would regret it all his life. She knew it would be a difficult pilgrimage for him to make and his look warned her to drop it, but she couldn't; she'd gone too far. 'I wouldn't get in your way. I'd just be there to take notes—act as your go-between. I could even help you source people to handle any necessary restoration work. You wouldn't have time for all that with all your other interests.'

'You seem to know a lot about me, Signorina Bannister.'

'I know you don't have a PA right now.'

Everything inside her tensed as Rigo went silent. The road out of her small town in Yorkshire was littered with returnees who had tried the big city and hurried back to the safety of home. Perhaps she should be doing that too, but she'd tried the big city—admittedly Rome with Rigo Ruggiero in it—and was in no hurry to return home.

'And you're telling me you can start immediately—without giving notice to anyone?'

Yes, she was burning her bridges. 'I have called the office and warned them I might not be back right away.'

'That's not a very good recommendation to a prospective employer, is it?' The look in Rigo's eyes told her how crazy this idea was, but then he added, 'I guess neither of us comes highly recommended where longevity of employment is concerned.'

He appeared to be battling with a decision, while her hands had balled into fists, Katie realised, slowly releasing them. Where had this crazy idea sprung from? She had never come across anyone like Rigo Ruggiero before, she reminded herself. He was still thinking. She had to interpret that as a maybe and, having taken the first step, found the second was much easier. Better to get things out in the open now. 'I do have one condition.'

'You're making conditions?'

Rigo's look pierced her confidence, but this was an all-important step in rebuilding her life. Yes, she was a small-town girl who was scarred comprehensively inside and out—and she should know her place—but retiring into the shadows would be a step back into the dark place she'd inhabited after the fire.

'Go on,' Rigo prompted impatiently.

'If we stay over in Tuscany—'

'I haven't agreed to you coming with me yet.'

'But you will,' she said, crossing her fingers behind her back.

'*If* we stay over?' he prompted.

'I'll need a place to stay.'

'Of course you will.'

'A separate place to stay…' Her face was growing hotter every second.

'Separate from me, do you mean?'

She heard the faint derision in his voice. 'That is correct,' she said tightly, feeling like that certain someone had come back to stand on her throat.

Rigo barked a laugh. 'Why?' he demanded. 'Don't you trust yourself alone with me, Signorina Prim?'

He was a busy man. Why was he making this hard for her? He needed a PA. And as he stared into Katie's pale, passionate face, he knew he wanted her to go with him. 'Well? What are you waiting for?' he snapped, frowning impatiently. 'Grab your bag, and let's go.'

Katie hadn't realised Rigo's idea of a trip to Tuscany would include a sleek white executive jet, which he piloted into Pisa Airport. Scurrying alongside him as he strolled through the terminal building without any of the usual formalities was another eye-opener. Next he introduced her to what seemed like an acre of cream calfskin in the back of a limousine. His chauffeur did the rest, driving them seamlessly through the exquisite Tuscan countryside, while she felt her thigh ping with the proximity of Rigo's thigh and fretted about sleeping arrangements.

Was she mad suggesting this? Dull little Katie Bannister off on a jolly with her drop-dead-gorgeous boss? What surprised her even more was that Rigo had accepted her offer to work for him—temporarily, of course. And now he was sending her senses haywire. She risked a glance his way as the car swept round a bend.

'Look, Katie…that palace on the hill is the Palazzo Farnese.'

Katie looked, but what she saw did not match Rigo's tone of voice. One of the ice-cream-cone-shaped towers looked as if it had been attacked with a battering ram, and to her eyes Rigo's inheritance looked more like a fat toad squatting on the top of the hill than a fairy-tale *palazzo*.

'It's a jewel, isn't it?' he breathed.

Katie hummed, trying not to sound too noncommittal. True, the hill the *palazzo* stood upon was lush and green, and had it been in good order the *palazzo* would indeed be set on the brow of that hill like a jewel. She set her imagination to work. It wasn't so hard. In some places where the passage of time had been kind the ancient stone glowed a soft rose-pink in the late-afternoon sunlight, and there were tiny salt-white houses clustered around the crumbling walls. Yes, it could be called beautiful—if you squinted up your eyes and tried to picture how the *palazzo* might look after a world of renovation—but oh, my goodness, how would Rigo react when they finally arrived?

'My family home…' Rigo's voice betrayed his excitement. 'I haven't been back for years…'

And years and years, Katie thought, trying not to imagine Rigo's disappointment when he moved past this nostalgia for a childhood that had ended with Carlo's arrival on the scene. Strangely, though she had no emotional involvement with the *palazzo*, it called to her too. She was bewitched and could already picture the rooms, which she imagined to have high vaulted ceilings, when they were loved and cared for. She knew instinctively the *palazzo* was worth saving. Monuments to another time were rare and precious and she could never dismiss one out of hand. How she would love to take a hand in restoring it…

And with her sensible head on she had an open ticket home if the job didn't work out.

Having driven up to the grounds, they entered through some ornate gates. A little shabby perhaps but that only added to their charm. They would need checking, of course, to make sure they were safe. She made a note. A gracious drive lay ahead of them, lined with stately sentinels of blue-green cypress. Well, at least those wouldn't need trimming, she thought, noting the overgrown flower beds and thinking of the work needed there. As the limousine swept on she could see it was all very grand—or had been at one time. Crenellated battlements scraped a cloudless cobalt sky and each conical tower, damaged or not, wore a coronet of cloud. 'It's magical,' she murmured.

'Let's hope so.'

Rigo's tone of voice suggested he had ditched the rose-coloured spectacles, and for that she was glad. And the setting was perfect. A limpid silver lake lay behind the *palazzo*, while the ghost of a formal garden could still be seen at the front amongst the weeds. To reach the main entrance they crossed a vast cobbled courtyard, which fortunately had survived intact, and as they passed beneath a stone arch she noticed a royal crest carved into the stone. Her heart juddered to see the same rampant lion engraved on Rigo's father's ring. That royal seal only put another wedge between them.

Rigo saw her interest and dismissed it. 'Everyone's son's a prince in Italy,' he said. 'Look on it as a benefit,' he added dryly. 'You can have a whole royal apartment to yourself.'

She smiled thinly and gave a little laugh. That was what she'd wanted, wasn't it?

CHAPTER TWELVE

ONCE upon a time she had believed in fairy tales, but that was before the fire. She knew Rigo only wanted her for her organised mind with the same certainty she knew this visit would be a disappointment for him. She was in serious danger of falling in love with him, Katie realised as the chauffeur slowed the car.

A group of uniformed staff was waiting for them at the top of the steps. They looked a little anxious, Katie thought, hoping Rigo would reassure them. Her heart was thundering as the limousine slowed to a halt. This was awful. She couldn't bear to think of Rigo disappointed or the staff let down. From start to finish this whole business was proving more disturbing than she could possibly have dreamed.

But Rigo seemed to have come to terms with the damage to the palazzo and put his disappointment behind him. 'I'm home,' he said, seizing hold of her hands.

He quickly let them go.

She followed him out of the car, registering more alarm now she could see how many twinkling windows were broken. She was still calculating the damage when she heard Rigo groan. Following his gaze, she felt like groaning too. A crowd of squealing fashionistas had started pouring out of the doors, pushing the hapless staff aside as they fought to be the first to greet Carlo's brother. These must be Carlo's friends, Katie realised, only now they were anxious to transfer their affections to Rigo.

'Hold this, will you?'

Thrusting a suitcase-sized handbag into Katie's arms, one of the older, immaculately groomed women elbowed her way through the scrum to reach Rigo, who was handling everyone with charm and patience, but as the woman reached his side and launched herself at him he frowned and turned around to look for Katie.

'You should have waited for me,' he said, coming immediately to her side. 'And whose is this?' he demanded. Removing the handbag from Katie's grasp, he dumped it on the ground. Putting his arm around Katie's shoulders, he shepherded her up the steps.

It didn't mean a thing, Katie told herself as her heart raced. Rigo was a very physical man for whom touching and embracing were second nature—a man who radiated command. Seeing her on the outside of the group had simply stirred his protective instincts.

She stood by his side at the top of the steps as he gave an ultimatum. His Press office would issue a further statement, he said, and in the meantime he was sure everyone would respect his grief and go home.

Smiles faded rapidly. People looked at each other. Then they looked at Katie and a buzz of comment swept through the group. Katie's cheeks reddened as she imagined what everyone must be saying—it ran along the lines of, what was a man like Rigo Ruggiero doing with a woman like her? She didn't have a clue either, if that helped them.

Rigo didn't appear to care what anyone thought, and chose to neither explain nor to excuse her presence.

Everyone saw a different side of him, Katie realised, from the Press, who loved to photograph him, to the hangers-on, who hoped to gain something by being here. She had seen his fun side and wondered how many people had seen that. Right now he was all steel and unforgiving. And if she'd only stopped to think—if these people had only stopped to think—they would all have known that a playboy could never have built up the empire Rigo had. She was as guilty as they were of being distracted by his dazzling good looks and his charm, but she had learned that to underestimate him was a very dangerous pastime indeed.

He went straight from this announcement to introduce himself to the staff and to reassure them. He insisted Katie accompany him for this and he introduced her as his assistant. No one seemed to think this the slightest bit odd and she received some friendly smiles.

Rigo looked magnificent, Katie thought as he returned to the top of the steps to be sure his orders were being carried out to his satisfaction. A Roman general couldn't have had better effect. Hope was already blossoming on the faces of his staff, and a very different look had come over the faces of Carlo's friends.

'We have to be a little patient,' Rigo confided in her, leaning close. 'Everyone has yet to learn that I am a very different man from my brother.'

'I think they may have guessed that,' Katie ventured.

'Your luggage and belongings will be packed and brought out to you,' Rigo announced to those who still refused to believe the gravy train had reached the station. 'Meanwhile, please feel free to enjoy the beauty of the grounds.'

But not the *palazzo*, Katie guessed as a groan went up.

'Come—' his face was set and hard as he turned to her '—we have work to do.'

The power emanating from Rigo was both thrilling and concerning. Even as Katie's hand strayed to trace the pattern of Rigo's breath on her cheek she could not shake the feeling that the inside of the *palazzo* was going to be worse than the outside. Wouldn't he need time alone to deal with his feelings? 'Maybe you'd like space?' she suggested.

'Space?' He looked at her as if she were mad.

'Some time alone? I'm sure I'll have no trouble finding somewhere to stay in town—'

'I thought you worked for me?'

'Of course—'

'Then why would you stay in town? This isn't a holiday, Signorina Bannister.'

'I didn't—'

'Did you bring a notebook?'

This was another side of Rigo—ruthless and without the playboy mask. He walked straight in while she hesitated on the threshold. Beneath her boxy jacket the tight skin on her back had begun stinging with apprehension, but for the first time in a long time she ignored it and started jotting notes: 'Replace damaged architrave…sand down and re-polish entrance doors…replace broken tile just inside the door. Replace all floor tiles,' Katie amended, feeling a chill grow inside her. At her side Rigo had gone quite still.

He swore in Italian. 'This is bad. And if you're still worrying about sleeping arrangements, don't.'

Rigo was in a furious temper, Katie realised, as well he might be, considering the abuse of his ancestral home.

'Whatever the state of this building,' he assured her in a snarl, 'you'll have a lock on your door and at least a mile of corridor between us.' And I wouldn't touch you with a barge-pole, his expression added viciously.

She held her ground and Rigo's stare. She had to believe

his anger wasn't directed at her. So her precious chastity would remain intact—that was what she wanted, wasn't it?

Yes, but not like this, not with Rigo treating her like the enemy.

Standing in the centre of what must once have been a gracious vaulted hall was heartbreaking, even for Katie. They had moved from the seductive heat of Tuscany, from air drenched in sunlight and laced with the heady scent of honeysuckle and roses, into a dank, dark space that reeked of decay. Spilled wine marked what must have once been an elegant marble floor and there were even cigarette butts trodden carelessly into the tiles.

'*Dio,*' Rigo murmured softly at her side.

If he had been anyone else, she would have reached out and grasped his hand to show her support, but she knew he didn't want that. His rigid form forbade all human contact. How would she feel if the beautiful home she remembered from her childhood and had longed to see again turned out to be a crumbling ruin that Carlo's friends had treated like an ashtray?

But a lot of the damage was superficial, Katie concluded as she stared around. She guessed there must have been one heck of a party in anticipation of Rigo's arrival, which made everything look so much worse. But there was some structural work to do as well… She made a note.

Rigo's face reflected both his anger and his agony. He looked on the point of walking out. She could sympathise with that. There had been many times when she had wanted to give up after the fire, and here in the *palazzo* it must seem as if the last remnants of Rigo's childhood had gone up in flames.

'*Vero*…I knew it was too good to be true,' he murmured. 'Now you can see my stepbrother's true nature and his legacy to me.'

As he raked his hair with stiff, angry fingers she could no longer resist the impulse to reach out. 'Rigo, I'm so sorry—'

'I don't need your pity,' he snapped. 'We're going back to Rome. I'm going to put the *palazzo* on the market—'

'And turn your back on it?' She was acutely aware that members of staff were hovering uncertainly in the background.

'I'll do what I have to do.'

'Rigo.' She chased him to the door. 'Don't you think you should—?'

'What?' he demanded furiously. 'Why can't you leave me alone?' He lifted his arm, shunning her concern, but the murmur of a worried staff was still ringing in her ears. 'No—wait,' she said, seizing his arm.

Rigo stared coldly at her hand on his arm. She slowly removed it. Here in this derelict *palazzo*, surrounded by old memories and faded glory with a battalion of servants watching them, she was more out of place than she had ever been, but someone had to try and reach Rigo. 'So Carlo wins—'

'He's already won.' Slamming his fist against the ruined door, Rigo leaned his face on his arm and fought to control his feelings. A long moment passed before he raised his head again. 'Call a meeting of the staff.' He sucked in a steadying breath before adding, 'Tell them I'll meet them here in the hall in two hours' time. And please reassure them,' he continued in a voice that was devoid of all expression, 'that before I go back to Rome they will all be taken care of.'

But who would take care of Rigo? Katie wondered. Seeing his childhood home reduced to a ruin had ripped his heart out. She knew how that felt too. 'Where will you go now?' she said, unconsciously clutching her throat.

'To find my driver. To make certain he has some rest and refreshment before we return to Pisa—'

'To fly to Rome?'

'Yes.' Distractedly he wiped a hand across his face.

'Don't you have to draw up a flight plan?' He needed time to get over this shock before he piloted a plane—before he decided what to do. She was looking for something, anything that would give him time to think.

Rigo shook his head as if to say, don't concern yourself with such things, and his next words proved to be the final nail in the coffin of her dreams. 'There's no job for you here, as I'm sure you've worked out. Please accept my apologies for a wasted journey,' he added stiffly. 'My driver will, of course, take you to the airport so you can catch the next flight home.'

Home…

The sound of the battered door slamming heavily into place behind him brought more plaster off the walls, but even as Katie turned to look around and saw the group of people waiting for her to reassure them she experienced something she couldn't put a name to. It was uncanny, almost like a sixth sense, but she felt as if she was already home.

CHAPTER THIRTEEN

THE servants were whispering and casting anxious glances Katie's way. Tears stung her eyes when she realised many of them were armed with sweeping brushes, buckets and mops. She crossed the hall, intending only to deliver Rigo's instructions about the meeting, but seeing all those worried faces triggered something inside her. 'Do you have a spare brush?' she said instead to the housekeeper. 'If we all pitch in,' she explained in Italian, 'this won't take so long…'

There was no need for words—no time for conversation from that moment on. There was just concentrated effort from a small team of people including Katie, all of whom were determined to give the grand old *palazzo* a second chance. The Palazzo Farnese might have been brought to its knees by Carlo Ruggiero's lack of investment and care and his friends' rough treatment of it, but everyone sensed this could be a turning point if they worked hard enough.

When the old hall smelled fresh and clean Katie made some discreet enquiries about where Rigo had gone.

'After speaking to his driver he went to the leisure suite,' the housekeeper told her. 'I took the precaution of locking it,' the older woman added, touching her finger to her nose as Gino had. This brought the first smile of the day to Katie's face. 'Very sensible,' she agreed.

Rigo's concern for his driver had obviously delayed their departure, so this was her chance.

'I would not allow those people near the swimming pools,' the housekeeper confided in Katie, 'and the new master has chosen to swim in the indoor pool today.'

The new master? Katie thought of the crest on the arch and on the ring. Here, Rigo wasn't Signor Ruggiero, the infamous international playboy, but someone else entirely. 'The new master?' she prompted.

'*Sì,*' the housekeeper said with pride. '*Principe Ruggiero. Principe Arrigo Ruggiero.*'

Arrigo? Prince Arrigo? 'Ah, yes, of course,' she said. The housekeeper might think her a little slow on the uptake, but it was better to be sure of her facts. And never mind that he was a prince, it was Rigo's state of mind Katie was most concerned about.

Thanking the housekeeper and the rest of the staff for all their help, she left the hall in search of him. She had to know he was all right. She had to let Rigo know he wasn't alone and that she'd stay by his side until he sorted this mess out.

Katie stood in the shadows, watching Rigo power down the length of the pool. He had dropped his clothes on the side and hadn't even stopped to turn on the light, though there was lighting in the pool. The luminous ice-blue water was a perfect frame for the dark shape slicing through it and she was fascinated by Rigo's strength and by his magnificent body. His powerful legs pounded the water into foam, while his sculpted shoulders gleamed bronze as they broke the surface. They were the powerhouse for his punishing freestyle stroke, though every part of him was involved.

And every part of him was naked.

She should turn and walk away, but she couldn't; she didn't

want to. She remained motionless, watching, until Rigo finally cruised to the end of the pool.

Now she really must go…

But the moment came and went and she still hadn't moved.

Rigo sprang out. Water fell away from his hard-muscled frame. Every inch of him was in gleaming, spectacular focus. She remained riveted, staring, learning more about a man's body than she could have imagined. Rigo naked was even more perfect than Rigo clothed…so perfect Katie's scars tingled a reminder that she was not.

'Signorina Bannister?'

His husky voice surrounded her. She shrank as he padded towards her. She couldn't move. She was trapped in the beam of his stare.

'What are you doing here?' he demanded.

She lacked the guile to lie. 'Watching you.' She was careful to stare straight into his eyes, but she could feel his sexual energy invading her. She wasn't afraid. If he had caught her without her clothes she would have been terrified, Katie realised. But shouldn't Rigo be making some attempt to cover up? Was it possible to lack all inhibition? Her body thrilled to think all things were possible for him. But not for her, the scars on her back gave her a stinging reminder.

'Forgive me,' he mocked softly as he came to stand in front of her. 'I would have worn swimming shorts had I expected a visitor.'

'I'm sorry to intrude…'

She was about as sincere as he was. She would never forget these few minutes at the side of an unlit swimming pool. Every craving nerve she had was on fire. She would try to store that feeling. Before this she hadn't understood that such levels of arousal were even possible. The pool lights were reflected in Rigo's eyes, casting forbidding shadows on his rugged face. 'I was worried about you,' she confessed awkwardly.

'Worried about me?'

He sounded amused. Heat grew inside her as he continued to stare at her. Why didn't he walk away? Why didn't she?

Because her bones had turned to honey...

She was slow to react when he moved and her heart drummed a warning, but all he wanted was the towel he'd left on a chair. Relief coursed through her when he snatched it up, but he only used it to wipe his face and left his naked body on full view.

Having dried his face, he drew the towel back over his hair and rubbed it with fluid, lazy strokes. Water-heavy hair caught on his stubble and meshed with his eyelashes, and it seemed forever before he looped the towel around his waist.

'You were watching me for quite some time, worried *signorina*,' he murmured. 'Did you learn anything?'

His eyes were challenging and amused. It came home to her then how much older Rigo was, and how much more experienced and sophisticated. She was little more than a trembling wreck, and had no idea how to behave in these circumstances. 'You swim well,' she ventured.

His short laugh displayed strong white teeth and one inky black brow peaked, but his mouth remained hard and his eyes were watchful. He was fresh from the shock of discovering what had happened to his childhood home, she reminded herself, and had been swimming to exorcise those demons.

But he still had energy to burn...

'You're blushing,' he said.

'How can you see in this light?'

Reaching out, he traced the line of her cheek. 'I can feel the heat coming off you...'

Her swift intake of breath sounded unnaturally loud. 'It is

very warm in here…' She gazed about in a pathetic attempt to distract him.

Rigo's low voice pulsed with intent. 'I don't think it's that sort of heat I can feel. Well, *signorina*?' he pressed. 'There must be something other than my swimming technique that kept you fascinated…'

Mutely, she shook her head. It was blood heat in the leisure suite and almost dark. Just the pool lights shimmering behind her like dots of moonlight on a lake. She felt cornered by a powerful predator, a predator she had sought out, and now her reward was to be wrapped in a cloak of arousal as she waited to see what would happen next.

The darkness concealed her flaws, and with Rigo's powerful body changed to shadowy imprecision in that darkness they could almost be two equals meeting here. It was a compelling fantasy in which she longed to lose herself, and as the pool room shrank around them she swayed towards him.

'Careful,' he murmured, putting warm palms on her upper arms, but only in a steadying gesture, 'you're very close to the edge of the pool…'

Still the child. Ever the innocent. Would he never see her any other way?

And shouldn't she be relieved about that?

She made light of it. 'Sorry…I didn't realise—I can hardly see anything in this light.'

Lies. All of it. She had seen every part of him, including the tattoo on his hip. 'I only came because I'm worried about you,' she said again. 'I called the meeting.'

'Good,' Rigo murmured.

His concentration on her hadn't wavered and his watchful eyes bathed her in heat. As he eased onto one hip she was consumed by the longing to touch him.

'Why don't you—?'

'Why don't I what?' she blurted guiltily.

'Why don't you tell me the real reason you came here?'

She heard the faint amusement in his voice. If only he would stop staring down at her. 'I already said—you had a shock, the will—'

'My brother and I were practically strangers.'

Katie's mouth felt dry as Rigo continued to stare down at her. 'The *palazzo*…' She was grasping at straws, they both knew it. She gasped as Rigo coiled a long hank of her hair around his finger. It must have escaped her bun while she was cleaning.

'The only distress I feel,' he assured her, 'is knowing my stepbrother wasted his life—'

'It doesn't have to be a wasted life.' She gazed up. 'You could change that.'

He laughed and let her go. 'You will learn that it is point-less looking back and wishing things might have been differ-ent. They are as they are.'

She had not expected him to move so fast, or to slip his hand into her hair again, and to make the next move cupping her head. 'The knack is in learning to move on, Katie…'

Their faces were very close and he was staring at her intently. 'Rigo…'

'What?' he murmured, drawing her gaze to his lips.

'You could stay here at the *palazzo* and make things right for everyone…' She couldn't forget the faces of the servants waiting hopefully for news.

'Delaying tactics,' he breathed with his mouth only a whisper from her lips.

Perhaps, Katie admitted silently, though her concerns for the people who lived here were real enough. And now they had reached the point she had longed for she was fright-ened—frightened she would disappoint him. How could she not when Rigo was perfection—when he had taken one look at the flawed *palazzo* and turned his back on it? 'You don't strike me as the sort of man who walks away from problems.'

The mood changed as she spoke. The heavy, erotic beat fell silent and was replaced by humour, at least in Rigo's eyes.

'I thought I told you, no counselling?' he said.

'Sorry…' She eased her neck as he stepped back. Would she ever forget his touch? 'I wouldn't dream of advising you—'

'I think you would,' he argued. 'I think you do a lot of dreaming, Signorina Bannister. I think you dream and want and need as much as anyone else.'

Breath shot from her lungs as Rigo seized hold of her.

He wanted her. Wanted her? He wanted to lose himself in Katie Bannister. He wanted to bask in her goodness and have it heal him. To begin with he'd been amused by the fact that Katie had worried about him enough to come and seek him out, but now he remembered that no one had ever done that for him before. And then he saw the hunger in her eyes matched his own and the time for restraint had passed.

There was no subtlety. As he slammed her against his hard warmth and his towel hit the floor he made no attempt to retrieve it.

Katie's senses had sharpened in the darkness to the point where she could smell the water on Rigo. She pressed against him, believing she was someone else—someone flawless, bold and hungry. She might be falling deeper into the rabbit hole and leaving reality behind—and maybe she should try to pull things back, but she didn't want to, and her body wouldn't cooperate, anyway. It was swollen with need, moist and ready, and so instead of pulling away from Rigo, she raised her face to his.

'Needs are nothing to be ashamed of, Katie. Even I have

them. I understand you, Katie,' he assured her. 'I know everything you feel.'

In that case he'd be ready to catch her when her legs buckled. Did he have any idea how hungry she was for this—how desperate for his touch? Did he know where and exactly how she wanted him to touch her? Her eyes were shut. She was barely breathing. She was suspended in an erotic net, and was totally unprepared when he pulled away.

The ache morphed into real physical pain. It took her a moment to realise Rigo's actions were so fluid he hadn't left her, but was kneeling on the hard tiles in front of her.

'No.' Her voice clearly said yes. As he lifted her skirt she clutched his shoulders for support.

'Yes,' Rigo murmured, burying his face.

An excited whimper ripped the silence as she unashamedly edged her legs apart. She was greedy for sensation, for experience, for him. Having taken the first step, she was ready to fly.

'Relax, worried *signorina*,' Rigo murmured, 'there's no rush.'

She could hear him smiling in the darkness.

CHAPTER FOURTEEN

HER heart was pounding so hard she couldn't breathe. Her wildest fantasy was coming true. Held firmly by Rigo, she was trapped, not by his grasp, but by her own overwhelming need. She didn't move, couldn't move, because she didn't want to. She craved fulfilment and satisfaction and a door into that world that had always been closed to her. She wanted everything Rigo was prepared to give her. She wanted to climax—and not once, but many times. She wanted this erotic dream to last forever and for reality to fade away. Closing her eyes, she bathed in darkness where there were no scars and only sensation registered. Consequences? What were they?

She sighed with disappointment as he started to stand up, but he took his time as if imbibing her scent on the way up. It thrilled her—aroused her even more. His face was only millimetres distant from her own, and her body was crying out for more contact between them. Swinging her into his arms, he lowered her down onto one of the recliners facing the pool, where silence enveloped them.

She blinked as he switched on the lamp by the chair.

'I want to see you come—'

'No.' She wasn't ready for that.

'Yes,' he argued steadily.

She was painfully self-conscious as he pressed her back against the cushions.

'Relax,' he said.

She was out of the dream and back to reality. This was embarrassing and wrong. She would regret it in the morning.

In the time it took to think that, he had pushed her skirt back to her waist, removed her underwear and lifted her legs to rest them on his shoulders.

She was completely exposed. Cool air brushed her most heated self as Rigo cupped her bottom in warm, strong hands, and instead of pulling away she settled down. Moments later he found her with his tongue and with his lips and with his fingers, rough stubble scratching the insides of her thighs, pleasure and pain intermingling. She hit a wall of pleasure and that wall gave way, drawing her deeper into a world of the senses where reality could not intrude. She bucked wildly. He held her in place. She screamed with abandon as he tipped her into the abyss, and while she was moaning with amazed contentment he kept her safe in his arms until the last flicker of sensation had subsided.

'Greedy girl,' he murmured.

With some satisfied sounds she was ready to fall silent. Language was a civilised pursuit and there was nothing civilised about her feelings for him. She was spent, exhausted, satiated—

And then she noticed the fire in Rigo's eyes. He was neither spent, exhausted nor satiated.

She jerked away as a hot stream of panic filled her. He didn't attempt to follow as she clambered awkwardly away from him. 'I'm sorry—'

'So am I. What are you ashamed of, Katie?'

'Nothing.' She spoke too fast and Rigo's eyes narrowed with suspicion. 'Sorry,' she said again, backing away. 'I don't know what I was thinking—'

'That we were two consenting adults, maybe?' he suggested in a voice that was calm while the expression in his eyes was anything but.

And who could blame him? Katie thought. She had led him to this point and then pulled away. 'I know what you must think of me—'

'You have no idea,' he assured her. Springing lightly to his feet, he collected his robe from the back of a chair and shrugged it on, belting it securely. 'So, Signorina Prim?' His voice had lost all warmth. 'What do you hope to get out of this?'

Rigo's expression frightened her. 'Nothing.'

'Nothing? So you haven't been leading me on in the hope of landing a greater prize?'

He wasn't talking to her, she felt instinctively, but to the woman who had taken his father from him, and to the many women who saw Rigo as the ultimate prize. 'No, of course I haven't been leading you on. Rigo, you're upset—you're not thinking straight—'

'Don't mistake me for one of your hard-luck causes—' dipping down, he scooped up her underwear from the floor. '—and don't forget these.'

He threw them at her, only for her to fumble and drop the dainty briefs she had bought in Rome.

'Pick them up,' he snarled. 'You might need them when you identify your next target.'

And with that he turned his back on her and stalked away.

He took the private staircase from the leisure suite to his rooms. The episode with Katie Bannister had sickened him. He knew who and what she was, just as he knew himself. This will, this so-called legacy, had undermined the man he had become and had left him feeling tainted by everything he had

vowed to leave behind. Seeing his childhood home dese-
crated had done exactly what Katie said. It had rocked his
world and he wasn't thinking straight.

Shouldering his way through the door, he entered his room
pacing and didn't stop until he had reasoned his motives
through on every point. He had encountered just about every
ruse to capture his interest and reel him in and was always on
his guard. Katie had reaped the whirlwind. Her appetite was
undeniable, but when he weighed that appetite against her
naïvety, or the shock on her face when she realised the road
they were on led to penetrative sex, he knew she was innocent.
So she had splurged on some decorative underwear. Did he
begrudge her even that small luxury?

Anger, regret and frustration had coagulated into one ugly
mass, he concluded. Seeing the *palazzo* brought to ruin hadn't
just shaken him to his foundations, it had filled him with un-
natural energy—or just plain fury, maybe. Whatever the
cause, he had needed an outlet for that energy and had chosen
badly. He should have stuck to swimming, he mused, smiling
bleakly. He could never give Katie Bannister what she wanted
and deserved, which was a loving husband and babies, a
home, romance, a happy-ever-after ending. Thanks to him she
had lost her innocence tonight. But perhaps it would keep her
safe from men with fewer scruples than he.

Stripping off his clothes, he took a long, cold shower
before swinging naked into bed. He wasn't going anywhere.
He was staying until this mess was sorted out. As Katie hoped,
he had embraced his legacy. He would take a negative and
make it positive. He would drink from Carlo's poisoned
chalice—but Principe Arrigo Ruggiero Farnese would not be
making any more mistakes.

He woke at dawn after a restless night. One face had held
sway in his mind, but she would hate him now. He turned his

thoughts to practical matters he could do something about and went straight to examine the north tower, where he found the roof caved in. But it could be fixed. Having survived centuries, the old place would stand a few more knocks before it surrendered.

It wouldn't be easy to restore the *palazzo*, he concluded after further investigation, and it would take many years and a lot of money. Money he had, and he had the determination to set it right. He would oversee this project personally. He'd handled many major building works in the past, but they had been investments for his money rather than his heart. He consulted with architects who sent teams in, but he wasn't prepared to do that here. He would be the main point of contact. He couldn't allow anyone to interfere with the *palazzo* who didn't remember it as he did.

Swinging across a beam, he dropped lightly to the floor. It was time to persuade Katie Bannister to stay. He needed her clear thinking and organisational skills. She could coordinate the various teams—if she had the courage to stay after what had happened last night.

He went to the window in his room and pushed the rotten frame with the heel of his hand until it yielded. He had to breathe some fresh air. He looked down, searching for Katie. Something told him she'd be outside. Birds were singing— the sun was shining; it was Katie's kind of morning. Resting his hands on the cool stone, he looked in vain. Pulling back, he felt the wear of time. Like everything else the stonework required expert attention. He would ask her to find the best team of stonemasons to begin work right away—if she still worked for him.

She must work for him.

Last night he had been infected by a maelstrom of emotion, but today he could see clearly that it was an assistant he needed, not a lover. And if Signorina Bannister didn't work out he could always sack her like the rest. Meanwhile, he'd take a shower and get rid of this dust.

Last night the choice had seemed clear. She was going home. She had proved conclusively she wasn't cut out for this any more than she was cut out for her dead-end job in Yorkshire. Her encounter with Rigo had proved to be the worst humiliation of her life.

But the best sex.

Better than anything she could dream up, Katie conceded. But deeply humiliating; she'd never get past it. And as for Rigo? Trying to imagine what he must think of her made her shudder.

But, when she came down to breakfast and discovered a new mood of optimism sweeping the staff, she immediately put her own feelings on the back burner.

'You have to stay,' the housekeeper protested when Katie explained she was leaving. 'It's such a lovely morning,' the older woman pressed her. 'The best of the year so far.' And then the clincher. 'We have cleaned the outdoor swimming pool especially for you.'

Bare skin. Scars. More humiliation. 'But I don't—'

One of the maids stepped forward. 'We are about the same size, *signorina*,' she said shyly, 'and I have a new swimming costume I have never worn.'

As the young girl held it out to her Katie knew she couldn't refuse.

'You'd be quite alone, *signorina*,' the housekeeper quickly reassured her. 'I'll make sure everyone is kept away—'

'You're very kind—'

'And you're the first person to come here and give us hope,' the woman told her frankly.

Was she going to show her weakness now? She had to be strong for these people all the time, not just selectively.

'It would be such a shame to waste the day,' the maid said as the housekeeper nodded agreement.

The damaged skin on Katie's back tightened, but she would feel more than shame if she refused this kind gesture. 'If…if I was alone—'

'You have my word on it,' the housekeeper assured her.

The cool water felt like satin on her heated skin, and as sunshine warmed her shoulders any remaining cares she had floated away. This was the first time since the fire that she had stripped off outside the privacy of her own home and she was surprised to find the costume the young maid had lent her fitted her so well. She had Rigo's staff to thank for making this possible.

Submerging her face in the fresh, clean water, Katie basked in the unaccustomed luxury of having a whole swimming pool to herself. And what a swimming pool it was—if she had thought the *palazzo*'s leisure complex was like something out of a film, this outdoor pool was far more beautiful. Stern Doric columns marked the perimeter, while mosaics tempted her to look beneath the water to where a kaleidoscope of images told a story of ancient Rome, complete with gladiators and graceful beauties clad in flattering flowing robes. I want one of those glorious gowns, Katie thought, buying into the dream. She was beginning to believe she could forget anything swimming here.

The housekeeper had opened the shutters and folded them back, allowing him a clear view of the gardens and swimming pool. Drawn by the particular brilliance of the sunlight that day, he walked over to the window after his shower and stared out. His gaze was immediately drawn to the activity in the pool, where someone was preparing to dive in…

Katie…

She had already been swimming and her hair was slicked back. Her honey-blush skin gleamed like an impossibly perfect sculpture in the brilliant light. She had surprised him once again. He had always suspected she was concealing a stunning figure beneath her dowdy clothes—just how stunning had eluded him, he realised now. He already knew her legs were beautiful, but… A whisper from last night intruded on his thoughts. Could he forget? He had to forget—he had a pressing need for a PA and she'd make a great PA. But with her hair drawn back and her elegant profile raised towards the sky, there was no doubt she was one of the loveliest sights he had ever seen. He remembered their first telephone conversation, when her sexy voice had revealed so much about her. You could hear beauty in a voice. Why she dressed down almost to the point of disguise was Katie's business, but he couldn't deny he was curious. Pulling away from the window, he stretched his limbs. Even an hour without activity was an hour too long for him. He was restless with last night playing on his mind again. Katie's responses to him…her soft whimpers…her tremulous, yet passionate plunge into abandonment and pleasure—

Maybe a swim was what he needed too.

'No, Rigo, no…'

He stopped dead in his tracks. He had only walked halfway down the pool, but she was recoiling from him as if he meant her harm. The last thing he had intended was to frighten Katie, but the moment she caught sight of him she had catapulted out of the pool and now she was stumbling backwards with a towel clutched tightly to her chest.

'I didn't see you, Rigo,' she gasped.

Was he such a terrifying sight? It was certainly terror in her eyes. He took a step back with his hands raised, signalling his intention to come no closer. Still she backed away. If she didn't stop soon she'd fall over the sunbed—

He breathed a sigh of relief when she felt the bed behind her knees and stopped, but now she was feeling awkwardly behind her for a wrap she'd left there earlier, and only he could see she was in real danger of tumbling into the pool.

'No! Stay back!' she shouted in alarm when he moved to save her.

'What the hell's wrong with you? I'm not going to touch you.'

Ever again, he added silently. If this was Katie Bannister's reaction to him, imagine if they'd had sex.

None of this made sense. She'd seen him naked. She'd held him. He'd let her go without once trying to stop her. He was respectably attired this morning in swimming shorts with a towel slung around his neck. He couldn't understand her bizarre behaviour and was growing increasingly resentful. But still her safety was uppermost in his mind. 'Stay where you are before you fall in. I'm going to reach for your robe,' he told her firmly, 'while you don't move a single muscle. Do you understand me?'

He wasn't even sure she could hear him, so he put his promise into action, moving slowly and deliberately. 'And now I'm going to hand it to you.'

Part of him said this was ridiculous, while another part of him was too busy seeking an answer to the mystery to walk away. Katie, meanwhile, remained stock-still, staring at him in wide-eyed dread.

He held out her wrap at arm's length. She took it from him. Dragging it on, she belted it tightly, tweaking the edges as if not a single part of her could be on view.

Had last night done this to her? He would never forgive himself if that was the case, though he could fathom no reason why it should. She had been a willing partner all along, up to the point where a natural conclusion was facing them both, and then, because she for whatever reason had drawn back, he had let her go.

'When you've showered and dressed I'd like to see you in the library,' he said evenly. 'Anyone will tell you where that is. Say, twenty minutes—half an hour?' His look also added, if you still work for me? But he didn't labour the point.

He didn't stop walking until he reached the entrance to the *palazzo*, when he turned to see Katie still standing where he'd left her. He wondered if he would ever forget the look on her face. You would have thought she had been in danger of her life.

CHAPTER FIFTEEN

WHEN Rigo left her at the poolside it took her a long time to settle, mentally and physically. Since the fire she had longed to be invisible and had almost achieved that goal—until this trip to Rome, when Rigo had forced her to face reality again. Deep down, she was grateful to him. There was still such a lot of life to be lived. Even before the fire her appearance had placed her in the pigeonhole marked good girl, plain girl, quiet girl, studious girl, which did nothing to douse the fires inside her. Last night Rigo had been right to point out she had needs like everyone else. Her needs were exactly the same as all the pretty, vivacious girls with great figures and unblemished skin.

There had been one short interlude when she had found an outlet for her passion in training to be an opera singer. Music had given her a means of expression until the fire stole her voice away. She had never thought to experience passion again until Rigo proved her wrong. And now she was at another crossroads, Katie realised. She could go back to Yorkshire and pick up her old life, or she could stay on in Italy as Rigo's PA.

When she had buried her face in the hospital pillows and cried the first time she saw the scars on her back the doctors had told her she would have to be brave. Take it one step at a time, they had advised. Life was a series of steps, she had discovered since then. You could take them bravely, or you could refuse to take them at all.

So the past had got the better of her?

She wouldn't let it.

Twenty minutes after leaving Katie at the pool, he was tapping a pen on the table, wondering if she was going to turn up—and if she did, was he about to make the biggest mistake of his life? He hadn't imagined taking Katie out of her comfort zone would throw her so badly. Forget the sex—that was never going to happen. But where the job was concerned he had to know if she was up to working alongside him in Italy.

The door opened and he put down his pen as she walked in.

'I know this is a business meeting,' she said when his face registered surprise, 'but I thought—if we needed to scramble round the building…'

His surprise that she had come at all was instantly replaced by relief and admiration. It took some guts to climb back to a position of composure and responsibility when you had lowered your guard to the point where you appeared a gibbering wreck. 'Sensible outfit,' he agreed, wishing she wouldn't always wear everything so big.

Camouflage, he realised, remembering the voluptuous figure she'd revealed at the pool. But why did Katie always feel this overwhelming need to cover up? The plain tailored trousers and simple jumper were a great improvement on the boxy suit, but they were hardly flattering. Thinking of the PAs he'd hired in the past made him want to shake his head in bemusement—when he would have preferred them to keep their clothes on they couldn't wait to whip them off. 'Don't you have any other clothes with you? Jeans?' he suggested.

'Just one pair I bought when I went shopping with Antonia. I didn't want to spoil them.'

He curbed a smile. That simple comment touched him somewhere deep. He'd become a stranger to having one of anything years ago. He turned determinedly back to business. He was already dressed in off-duty jeans and a casual top and was ready for the dirty work ahead of them. 'So you're ready to start work?'

'Yes, I am,' she said, staring straight into his eyes.

He came around the desk to shake her hand. 'Welcome to the team.'

She liked the way Rigo could be strong and unemotional. She also didn't like it—and for his sake more than anything else. A man so easily divorced from emotion could end up lonely. But she wanted this job and Rigo's grip was firm and compelling. She wished with all her heart things could have been different between them, but they weren't different. She had to hold her nerve now so he would understand she had drawn a line under everything that had happened between them. 'I hope I don't disappoint you,' she said, noting that Rigo held her hand for precisely the right length of time an employer should hold the hand of an employee.

He smiled slightly. 'I don't think there's the slightest danger of that.'

When roused, don't stand in his way. Rigo waited for no one, Katie concluded as he strode off. Even her embarrassment had been refused time to ferment. He was out of the library and across the hall before she had pulled a pen out of her bag, and now her heels were rattling across the floor in hot pursuit. They were surrounded by priceless antiques and frescoes that wouldn't have looked out of place in the Sistine Chapel, and the scent of history competed with the strong smell of disinfectant from the recently cleaned floor and was a dizzying combination. Or was that the Rigo effect? She was going to work for him. She did work for him. She ran faster and almost collided with him at the foot of the stairs. He gave her no time to recover. Seizing her shoulders, he swung her around. 'Tell me what you make of this.'

Breath shot out of her lungs in a gasp as she followed his gaze up the stairs to take in the garish stair carpet. Truth? Or diplomatic lie?

'Come on, come on,' he pressed. 'I want a reaction—'

'It stinks.'

'That's what I think. What should we put in its place?'

A runner at most. Or, depending on what they found underneath, the naked steps. She told him. He agreed.

'Make a note.'

She did so.

Oh, this job was fun. She raced after him. Who else had a boss so big and hard and sexy, a boss who only had to look at her to fill her body with the zest for life—along with other things? She didn't mind running to keep up with Rigo's easy, loping stride, because if he stopped suddenly she had discovered that crashing into him was like crashing into a padded wall—and who wouldn't want to rest against that, and even writhe a little, given half a chance?

'Well?' he demanded, thumping the wall with his meaty fist. 'What do you think of this?'

'They've plastered over stone that might have been better left exposed.' She pressed her lips together as their eyes met briefly. Images of other things—more interesting, but just as hard as stone—made her cheeks blaze.

'Exactly,' he rapped, striding off again.

She sucked in a breath and refocused determinedly before hurrying after him.

'This is a recent addition too.' He disdainfully flicked a hand at some dismal curtains and strode on again.

She made a note to replace the hangings.

'This is a disgrace,' he snapped, moving her aside to examine a sleazy mural more closely.

'Sandblast it?'

He almost smiled.

'We'll need a historical architect to advise us on renovations,' he said, walking on. 'Take a note.'

Something in the tone of that voice doused her enthusiasm. He was beginning to take her for granted. '*You'll* need one,' she said. 'I don't know how long I'm going to be here—trial period,' she reminded him, chasing after him down some stairs. This wasn't turning out as she had expected. She wanted more out of life than taking notes. She wanted to be listened to, at the very least, even if her thoughts were later discarded. But had Rigo even heard her?

She was ready to renege on their deal, Katie realised. She had been invited to become part of a team, not a dictatorship. She would stay until Rigo found a replacement for her, but then she would go home and find some other, safer way to spread her wings.

'This is more like a casino than a valuable historical site,' he remarked, opening one door and slamming it shut with a bang. 'Make a note—'

'You make a note.' She shoved her notebook in his hand. 'You know what you want. Presumably you can write it down.'

She'd never thrown a temper tantrum in her life. Rigo paused to look at her. He let one beat pass, and then another. He made no attempt to take the pen and paper she was offering him. 'What do you think of the room?' he said mildly then.

She gritted her teeth. 'I think it looks more like a casino than a site of historical importance,' she ground out.

His lips tugged. Her body yearned. They walked on.

'This used to be a slate floor,' he observed, sounding more relaxed.

The mood was catching and, in spite of her reservations, she relaxed too; enough to carry out her own investigations. They had entered a second, dimly lit corridor leading off from the first and once again it was lavishly carpeted in hotel style. 'I think we'd better add a stone-floor specialist to the list.'

'I agree,' he murmured in her ear. There was humour in his gaze that did considerable damage to her composure. He walked on. 'It wouldn't surprise me to find a nightclub and a spa down here.'

'Could this be it?' Katie wondered, peering into a stale-smelling cavern. Judging by the heaped ashtrays and the litter of drinks, this was the room in which Carlo's friends had chosen to wait for them. 'I'll get round to clearing it up as soon as I can—'

'*You'll* get round to it?' He swung towards her. 'That's not your problem. Katie.'

Signorina Prim, Signorina Dull, had had enough. The demon temper had been roused and was still very close to the surface. She only had to remember working alongside Rigo's staff the previous evening for that temper to erupt into words. 'I might not be stylish and rich like you, but if there's one thing I do know about, it's cleanliness and order. Who do you think cleaned the hall? You have a wonderful staff if you chose to notice them.'

To her surprise Rigo didn't respond to her attack, and instead granted her a mocking bow. 'I can assure you my wonderful staff has already told me what you did here yesterday.'

'They did most of it—'

'You claim no credit?'

'Why should I?'

He gave her a look. 'Why didn't you ask me to help?'

Her only thought had been to start getting things in a better state for him. 'I didn't want to trouble you last night.' Blushing now, she quickly changed the subject, having convinced herself she neither needed nor wanted Rigo's praise. 'You were upset and so—'

'You're making excuses for me?' he suggested mildly.

There was that flash of humour again in his intense green gaze and she hungered for more of it. There was silence while they studied each other's faces with new understanding. It was no longer Rigo Ruggiero, infamous playboy confronting Katie Bannister, poorly paid messenger girl with a hopeless taste in suits, but a man and a woman who each had the same goal.

But don't get too carried away, Katie warned herself, breaking eye contact first. A leopard doesn't change its spots that easily. A maxim that could apply to both of them, she conceded as Rigo resumed his inspection.

'This room will have to be gutted…'

And with that the spell that had so briefly held them was broken.

'In fact,' he added, 'all the rooms will have to be gutted—make a note.'

She did so, but this time there was a smile hovering round her lips. No wonder he couldn't keep his staff. 'It's only cleaning and redecoration,' she pointed out, but by the time she looked up from her notebook Rigo was out of sight.

Had he forgotten she was with him? Katie wondered when she found Rigo examining an electrical circuit box. 'Electrician?'

'Full check,' he confirmed. 'Our first goal must be safety for everyone, and then we must concentrate on bringing the *palazzo* back to its authentic state.'

'No earth closets, I hope?' she couldn't resist murmuring as he cast an eye over her notes.

'State-of-the-art plumbing. There's nothing better than a long, hot shower.'

As he looked to her for agreement she blushed again.

Opening a door at the far end of the corridor, he stepped outside. She followed, desperate to be free of all the conflicting emotions bottled up indoors. Gulping in the fresh, clean air, she exclaimed with pleasure and relief.

Rigo turned to look at her. 'How do you like the job so far?' he demanded.

She saw the irony in his eyes. 'I'm only here until you find a replacement.'

'Or I sack you.'

There was another of those long moments where they stared into each other's eyes. A breeze had whipped Rigo's hair into a fury, but his eyes were full of laughter as he raked it back.

She'd asked for this and she'd got it. Mad for him or not, she was under no illusion: Rigo wanted someone with an organised mind to take notes for him, just as he said. He needed her—not for all the reasons she'd like, but because she could keep life organised. She was a convenient choice, Katie reasoned as he dropped onto one hip. 'Are you coming or not?' he said.

'I'm right here.'

'Of course, you do realise if you prove satisfactory this could become a permanent position.'

'*If* I decide I want it.' She looked away so he didn't see her disappointment. Her dreams extended further than being his PA in a suit.

They spent the rest of the morning checking and discussing and formulating an initial plan of action, while she filled her notebook with notes. By lunchtime Katie could only conclude Rigo had some magic dust that had wiped the previous night's debacle from her mind. The incident at the pool also appeared to have been forgotten. It was better this way for both of them, Katie concluded; no tension, no agenda, purely business.

They joined the staff for lunch, all of whom were keen to put Rigo's plan for them into action right away. 'But run everything past me,' Rigo reminded Katie as he left her in charge. 'I've had enough surprises for one visit.'

She didn't doubt it.

CHAPTER SIXTEEN

KATIE'S face burned as she saw knowing smiles exchanged between the staff. Rigo had come back into the kitchen to tell her that two teams of men were waiting and he needed her right away.

'To take notes?' she suggested, avoiding his gaze.

'You're quick,' he murmured, ushering her out. 'One team is here to start work on the heavy cleaning,' he explained, 'so we don't put unnecessary pressure on the staff.'

'Good idea. And the other?'

'They're here to sort you out—'

'Sort me out?' Katie exclaimed.

Taking the pad from her hand, Rigo stuck it in the back pocket of his jeans. 'You won't need to take notes for this.'

'For what?' Katie's heart leaped into her throat as Rigo took her by the hand.

'If you're going to be working for me you'll need a new wardrobe of clothes—'

'To go rooting round the cellars with mice and spiders?'

'Your clothes are giving me eye-ache.'

'Well, I'm sorry if I—'

'You might be in Italy, but you don't have to dress like a *nonna*.'

Katie was too shocked to speak. A maiden aunt was one thing, but a grannie? Freeing her hand, she stood her ground. 'I'm hardly on show. And as I'm only here until you find a—'

'Think of it as your uniform,' Rigo interrupted, 'though, of course, I expect you to set a good example to the servants when you're off duty too—'

'And will you be buying them clothes?'

'I will, as it happens. It's about time they had something new, don't you think?'

He'd put her in an impossible position, but then Rigo was good at that.

'Rigo, wait—'

He stopped suddenly in the middle of the hall. Catching hold of her, he steadied her on her feet and stood back. Two groups of men were waiting at the far end of the hall—one team wearing overalls, the other in flamboyant suits. The overalls looked more appealing right now. She freed herself as discreetly as she could, conscious that even in a space as big as this sound travelled. As did sexual chemistry between two people. 'Even if I did work for you on a permanent basis, which I don't,' she told Rigo in an impassioned whisper, 'I have a perfectly serviceable suit—'

'That brown thing? Chuck it. Or, if I find it first, I'll chuck it out.'

'Fortunately it's already packed in my suitcase.'

'So you've decided not to stay?'

'I was ready to leave last night,' she admitted. 'I asked your driver if he would take me to the airport today.'

'Well, lucky for you I spoke to him too. And next time please do me the courtesy of speaking to me before you instruct my staff. Now, let's get on. None of these people want to be kept waiting. I can't think of a woman in the world who would turn down the chance to have the designers I have chosen create a look for her.'

'A mistress in the world, maybe.'

It was only a mutter but he heard her.

'Don't flatter yourself.'

Ouch.

'I'm merely extending the same courtesy to you I show to all the people who work for me—'

'And you can't keep any of them.'

She could always call a cab, Katie reasoned as Rigo's expression darkened.

'Those I don't want leave my employ.'

'So I have to earn the right to work for you?'

'You have to do the job you're paid for. That's reasonable, isn't it? There's a wonderful opportunity here if you want to be part of it. With the right team I can take Carlo's poisoned chalice and turn it into something wonderful—and that's all I'm prepared to say at the moment.'

'You're talking about something more than renovating the *palazzo*?'

'When my ideas are fully formed I'll let you know.'

'So you don't trust me, but you want me to work for you?'

'I'm saying confidentiality is an issue.'

'I'd need to know more.'

'When I'm ready.' And, when she still looked doubtful, his lips curved in a dangerous smile. 'Do you really need more time to get used to the thrill of working for me?'

Rigo's arrogance she could deal with, even his impossible behaviour she was getting used to, but when he played the humour card she was lost.

Just about. 'I can't afford to deal in riddles where my career is concerned,' she prompted, only to have Rigo close the matter with a decisive gesture. 'This will have to wait until you've seen your team. Come and show me when you've made your selection.'

'At most I need one plain and simple suit.'

Rigo shrugged. 'Your loss.'

And with that he left her to negotiate plain and simple with men for whom Katie guessed plain and simple was an abomination.

Katie was forced to admit she was wrong. As the designers discussed their ideas she realised their taste wasn't so far distant from her own—just in monetary terms. Unlike some men she could mention they were prepared to listen. When she asked for plain and simple they called it stylish and smiled. Once they had reassured her that all the measurements they needed could be taken over her clothes, she relaxed. They agreed on one tailored suit with both skirt and trousers to ring the changes, as well as three sharp shirts. They could dress her from stock, they admitted, to which she agreed immediately. It was both cheaper, and…well, truthfully, she couldn't wait to see what they had in mind.

So she did have a figure, Katie realised as she performed a twirl later in the privacy of her own room. It was a surprise to find she was a stock size and didn't even need an alteration, but then breasts were most definitely 'in' in Italy, where clothes made allowances for women with generous curves.

Left to her own devices she might have chosen something concealing, but the designers had insisted the jacket would hang off her shoulders if she chose a larger size. The elegant navy-blue tapered pencil skirt and matching short jacket with a sexy nipped-in waist made her look, well, if not glamorous—she could never be that—then, at least, something the right side of presentable. It was such a thrill to have some smart new clothes—and, as uniforms went, she conceded wryly, staring at the label in awe, this wasn't half bad.

The accommodation the housekeeper had chosen for her was another delight. It had survived the worst excesses of Rigo's brother and was the most beautiful suite of rooms Katie could imagine. The silks might be faded, as was the counterpane on the bed, but Katie had always loved shabby chic and this was the perfect example of it. She wouldn't change a thing in the room. Having everything pristine and new would take away from the *palazzo*'s charm. Any renovations would have to be carried out with the utmost sensitivity—though she had no doubt Rigo was more than capable of that. He was very different from his public face. The Press might think him a playboy, but that only showed how little they knew him.

She sighed as she gazed out across the formal gardens. She was more than a little in love with him even though much of Rigo was hidden behind whichever mask he had chosen to suit his purpose. She wondered what he was hiding and why—and what were these plans of his? He had decided to keep the *palazzo* and renovate it, but then he was going to use it for something he wouldn't tell her about. Would he ever trust her enough to tell her? And could she stay until he did?

He'd have to tell her if she was going to work for him, Katie reasoned, pulling back from the window. No employer could hide much from his PA. Was that why he'd sacked so many? Rigo was asking them to give blind loyalty to a man they knew to be ruthless and who would only tell them what he thought they should know. Would she put up with that?

Glancing at her watch, Katie realised it was time to show Rigo the outfits she had selected. Outfit, she corrected herself, smoothing the skirt of her new suit. So that shouldn't take up too much of his time—though what he would think of the sexy shoes the designers had insisted she must wear with the severely cut two-piece, she couldn't imagine. Well, she could. He would think her frivolous and extravagant and with very good reason. Lifting up a heel, she stared rapturously at the luscious crimson sole. The contrast with the black patent court shoe was both subtle and fabulous. She had never owned shoes like these in her life before and would have to pay Rigo back from her wages, which meant staying on—for a time. The shoes were worth it, Katie concluded.

Katie Bannister in high heels and designer labels—who'd have thought it? Katie Bannister, whose heart was beating like a jack-hammer, because she was going to see the man she loved, though Rigo must never guess how she felt about him.

He stood watching her as she walked across the hallway towards him. He noticed the way her hips swayed as if she had only recently become aware of her femininity. She loved her new suit. He loved to see her wearing it. He could tell she liked it by the way she moved. It was so good to see her standing straight, walking tall, hiding nothing.

He wanted her.

She hadn't seen him yet and so she knocked on the door of the library, where she expected to find him. Hearing no reply, she moved on towards the entrance to the leisure suite. He walked up behind her, hoping to surprise her, but something flashed between them and she turned. 'You look beautiful,' he murmured.

He heard her swift intake of breath. She remained quite still. 'Really beautiful…' He didn't touch her. He didn't want to spoil the moment as it shimmered between them. And then he noticed she was trembling.

'Do you really like it?' she said.

'More than you know…' He was sick of the pretence. He

was sick of Katie's lack of self-belief. He wanted the chance to help her rebuild it. He wanted her in his bed. She wanted him. She couldn't have made it more obvious. Her honey-coloured eyes had darkened to sepia and her parted lips offered him a challenge he couldn't ignore. Katie Bannister was changing faster than any woman he had ever known and the look of question, of adventure in her eyes mirrored his own. 'Now you've got the uniform,' he teased her, 'be sure you obey all my commands.'

'Until you sack me?' She refused to see the joke. 'I'll work in a team as you first suggested, Rigo, but I refuse to be the next in a long line of disposable dollies dressed for your amusement—'

'Is that what you think this is?' He gave the suit ensemble an appreciative once-over. 'And I thought you'd like it.'

'I do,' she admitted. Her eyes were wide and innocent, but there was a riot of activity behind them.

'Rome *and* Tuscany,' he tempted, sure that was an offer she couldn't refuse.

'I'll stick with the trial period we agreed on, thank you.'

'I need your organised brain on board.'

'I'm flattered,' she said dryly.

'I mean it. You're quiet, organised, discreet, quick-witted—'

'Biddable, do you mean?' she interrupted. 'Or just plain dull?'

'Dull? Who said quick-witted was dull?' Had the definition changed since the last time he used it? 'Work *with* me,' he tempered, keeping the bigger picture at the forefront of his mind.

'As what, Rigo? The perfect back-room girl?'

'You want to run the show?' he demanded with exasperation, planting his fist on the door above her head.

'Before I agree to anything I'd have to know exactly what's involved. That's reasonable, isn't it?'

Their lips were inches apart and he was tempted to take advantage of that and then tell her everything. But he was still developing the idea and his kids' club wasn't up for negotiation. It was and always would remain confidential—not for his sake, but for theirs. He wouldn't go out on a limb where that was concerned and he wouldn't put unfair pressure on Katie. 'I can't tell you yet—'

'But you expect me to throw up everything I have in England and move to Italy to work with you on a permanent basis on this…secret project?'

'I'm asking you to take a chance.'

'With you?'

He stared into her eyes and wondered how he had ever thought Katie Bannister a quiet little mouse. Passion lurked so close to the surface in both of them and her sweet wildflower scent was driving him crazy.

But he was not as innocent as she was.

'No, you're quite right,' he said, 'this would never work. I can't imagine what I was thinking.'

Rigo enjoyed provoking her. She knew that. Even so she was tempted to go along with his plan. He had injected danger into her life and she was addicted to it now. But could she work for him and feel like this? Could she do anything with a clear head until he finished what he had started last night? Sexual desire did not play by the usual rules. Clear thinking could vanish in an instant, leaving only the danger of desire.

'Shall we take this somewhere more private?' Reaching past her, he opened the door.

The door swung to, enclosing them in the sensual cocoon of the luxury spa. Rigo locked the door and handed her the key. Neither of them spoke; they didn't need to. Heat spread through her body until it came to a pulsing halt. Her lips were parted and her eyelids were heavy. She was ready and so was he. She could feel Rigo's breath on her face, on her neck, on her ear, his lips only millimetres away. They stood facing each other, staring into each other's eyes. When she was certain she could stand it no longer he drew her close. The relief was such she cried with pleasure. Her body was pressed hard against his and she could feel his erection throb and thicken as it strained against the fabric of his jeans. The more she tried to fight this Katie registered dizzily, the more she wanted him.

'So what would it take to bend you to my will?' he suggested wickedly.

'A miracle?' she countered, deliberately provoking him.

'A miracle?' he murmured. 'Or this…'

He claimed her mouth, teasing her lips apart—punishing her with kisses. As she responded he cupped her bottom and memories of sensation came streaming back. Was it only last night? How could she be so hungry? This wasn't decent— she would go mad. She was composed of sensation and need, she was all hunger, all mindless, searching, craving, desire. 'Oh, please…'

Briefly, he lifted his head to stare down at her.

'Please, touch me…' She was so swollen and aching. Winding her fingers through his hair, she dragged him close, demanding more, demanding everything he had to give her.

'Is this any way to behave?' he whispered with amusement.

'Now…' She cried out with frustration. 'Don't tease me…' Edging her legs apart, she gave him the most brazen invitation yet. She had to have him. She had to draw him deep inside her. It was a primitive imperative she had no will to resist. Her inhibitions were cancelled out by the demands of a body that craved his touch. She needed more contact, more touching and stroking, more pleasure. Memories from last night were too vivid for her to ignore this opportunity.

'Tell me what you want,' he taunted her softly. 'Direct me…'

'I want all of you now…'

'Explain.' His voice was stern. He held back.

'I want you to touch me again.' She said this in a clear and lucid voice. 'I want you to touch me exactly as you did before…'

'Exactly?'

'But this time I don't want you to stop.'

There were no more words spoken between them. Rigo undid the fastening on her skirt and let it drop to the floor. Her new lace briefs followed. She closed her eyes as he enclosed the luscious swell between her legs. The touch of him there was indescribable.

'More,' she insisted in a groan, clinging helplessly to him. 'Give me more—'

'Like this?'

'Oh, yes…'

But he was teasing her with almost touches. He would stroke her deliberately the way she liked and then return to a touch that was far too light.

'Don't tease me,' she begged, and as her legs buckled he took her weight.

Somehow her legs were locked around his waist, and as he freed himself and protected them both, he insisted, 'Use me.'

She gasped with shock as if the idea had never occurred to her. Rigo had given her the key to a new world, and one she had been longing to open since the moment they met. Taking him in her hands while he supported her, she touched him to her swollen flesh.

'Again,' he commanded.

CHAPTER SEVENTEEN

SHE used Rigo for her pleasure, not once, but many times, although there came a point where using him that way wasn't enough. As her hunger rose Rigo backed her against the wall. 'Yes,' she groaned, clinging to him. 'Yes,' she husked gratefully on a long note of satisfaction as he eased inside her. Still cupping her buttocks with one hand, he added to her pleasure with the other and as he thrust deeper, faster, she arced towards him, urging him on with impassioned pleas. She had never thought, dreamed anything could feel so good, but this was more than a craving; for the first time in her life she felt complete.

He had never known sex like it. She was insatiable. She was passionate. She was perfect. But for him this was only the appetiser and now he wanted the feast. He wanted to take Katie to bed and make love to her all night.

He had lost count of how many times she had climaxed by the time he withdrew. He did so carefully, making sure she was steady on her feet when he lowered her to the ground. Embracing her, once, twice, his heart throbbed with unexplored feelings. The next step had to be bed, but to his astonishment when he suggested it she pushed him away. 'Not again.' He shook his head, refusing to believe she could do this a second time.

'I can't—'

'What do you mean, you can't?' Drawing her close, he kissed her passionately, tenderly, but she wouldn't or couldn't respond. It made no sense. Anger grew inside him. She wanted him for sex—for instant gratification, but when it came to something deeper, more meaningful...

He had been used. A surge of disgust swept over him. Had he misjudged this? Was it all an act? Was Katie Bannister in love with someone else? He stepped back. Seeing his expression change, she reached out to him. 'Rigo, please—you have to believe me when I say there's a very good reason—'

'For sating yourself and moving on?' He shook his head in disbelief. He had only felt this level of betrayal once before, as a child whose pure love had been wasted on a man whose lust for a woman had taken precedence over love for his only son. 'Give me the key.'

Fumbling through her pockets, she finally found the door key and gave it to him.

Clutching it in his fist, he left the spa without a second glance.

As the door slammed behind Rigo Katie slowly crumpled to the floor. Burying her head, she sobbed in a way she hadn't been able to cry since the fire. She had never grieved for what she'd lost. She had never let the feelings inside her come out. Only her love for Rigo could open those floodgates. She had never felt anything as life-changing as this before—or directed so much loathing at her scars. She was crying because they could never be together and because sometimes it was easier to be strong than to break down, because being strong meant putting on an act, but when the mask dropped and there was just Katie Bannister facing up to her new life Katie wondered if she was strong enough or if too much had been lost.

Strong enough? Dry your eyes this minute, Katie's inner voice commanded.

Picking herself up from the cold tiles, she rebuilt herself breath by ragged breath. There was no reprieve, no easy way, because deep inside her was a determined little light that kept on shining however hard she tried to put it out. She would get over this. She would get over Rigo. She would go on living. Scarred or not, she knew there would always be problems. She could sit here on a hard floor in an empty spa, wailing for a past that had whistled away, or she could pick up her mental armour and go back into battle.

Which was it to be—wailing or winning?

She would do more than survive; she would make a difference.

'What's this?' Rigo stared at the letter Katie had just placed in his hand. They were in the library where she had found him pacing.

After what had happened in the spa she had no option but to do this. 'It's my resignation… You don't have to accept it, but I'll understand if you do.'

'That's very good of you.' He eyed her brown suit with distaste. 'So, are we right back where we started, Signorina Bannister?'

'Hardly.' She had barely finished the denial when Rigo's look communicated all he thought of her in wounding detail.

'I don't accept your resignation.' He handed the letter back. 'You agreed to stay until I could find a replacement.'

'That was before—'

'Before what?' he snapped.

She looked away, unable to meet his gaze.

'As you may be aware, I haven't had time to find a replacement for you yet. So I'd be grateful if you'd stay.'

He sounded so cold, so distant and, yes, so contemptuous. She flinched as he threw himself from his chair and stalked to the window, where he remained with his back turned to her, staring out. 'If I weren't so pushed...' he grated out, leaving Katie in no doubt that he would get rid of her the moment he could.

'I could resign. I still have my open ticket home—'

'You can do what the hell you want—and seem to do just that, from what I've observed.' Rigo's eyes were narrowed with fury and suspicion as he looked at her.

'I'm sorry—'

'Don't even go there.'

'You don't make it easy, Rigo.'

'I don't make it easy?' he demanded incredulously. 'You're guilty on that count too—and if it's easy you've come for you might as well leave now.'

Turn her back on him for ever? Face life with no possibility of seeing Rigo again? 'Is there any way we can work together now?'

'You tell me.'

Could he sound any more hostile? 'If we kept it on a strictly business footing?'

'Let me assure you right away there's no chance of anything else.'

Less than an hour ago there had been fire in those eyes. And now...

Digging her nails into her palms, she agreed to stay on. 'If you tell me what the job entails.'

'That's very good of you.'

'Rigo, please...I've said I'm sorry—'

'You're always sorry—maybe once too often.'

'I understand why you're angry with me—'

As she said this he made a sharp sound of disbelief. 'You understand nothing,' Rigo assured her. 'You're a child.'

And he, with all his Roman passion in full flood, was a formidable sight. She had never wanted him more or felt so distanced from him. Feet braced against the floor, fists planted on his tightly muscled hips, Rigo Ruggiero was a force she should run from as fast as she could before her heart was lost for good. 'If you won't accept my resignation—'

'Which I won't. We have an agreement,' he reminded her.

'Then will you tell me what you plan for the *palazzo*?'

'Do you really think I should trust you after what happened between us—not once, but twice?'

If they couldn't move past the sex there was no hope of a working relationship and if she was going to stay she had to do so with her head held high. The only way to do this was not to blush and shrink, but to challenge Rigo as he had challenged her. 'You threw down the gauntlet when you dared me to take a risk. I'm throwing that same gauntlet at your feet. Take a chance on me.'

Where had she come from, this female virago? Had he created her or were they equally guilty? Did they rouse such powerful feelings in each other that neither of them were capable of behaving as they should? He pointed to a chair. She sat while he paced. He was weighing up the potential of the *palazzo* for the scheme he had in mind—a scheme that would benefit his foundation—against his obligation to secrecy. Should he trust this woman? Could he trust her? What did his instinct tell him? 'I'm going to outline your contract,' he said, 'so if you would like to take a note…'

She hid a smile. He let it go. He dictated a letter to his legal team asking them to draw up a contract for Katie Bannister that gave her cast-iron guarantees.

She turned to look at him halfway through. 'I can't sign anything until I—'

He swore viciously in Italian. 'Must you argue every point? I want you to send the letter exactly as I have dictated it—'

'Don't I have any say in my own contract of employment?'

'Yes.' He was tired of playing softball. 'You can sign it or not. You can go back to Yorkshire and look for another job, if that's what you want, but I don't think it is. Am I right?'

She ground her jaw and came right back at him. 'I want a clause that allows for a time limit and fair notice to be given on either side—'

'A quick fix?' he suggested coldly. 'Is that the type of thing you deal in, Signorina Bannister?'

'Please don't turn me down out of hand. Try to see this from my point of view—'

His hackles stood on end. 'From your point of view? Isn't all this from your point of view? And what do you mean, don't turn you down out of hand? *Caro Dio*, what is this? I'm the one making the offer—'

'And making no allowance for my feelings—'

'You have too many feelings,' he roared, only to realise she was in tears. 'Don't play that card with me,' he warned, shaken to his core. 'I know your type—'

'My *type*?' she exploded, rallying faster than he could ever have expected. 'And what type would that be, Rigo?'

They were facing each other like combatants in a ring, but indignation gave way to amusement when it occurred to him that to any outsider Katie would appear by far the more dangerous of the two. With her hands balled into fists, her jaw jutting and mouth firm, her eyes blazing with the light of battle she was a magnificent sight, this woman of his—

His woman?

His woman.

The only woman he could ever want.

But his woman hadn't finished with him yet. Not by a long way.

'So I'm the type who can see you naked in a pool and make

the mistake of thinking we could share something special—'
She broke off. 'Oh, no, I forgot.' She held up her hand as if
to silence him, though he had no intention of saying a word.
He was content to let her continue this one-way argument
with herself and by herself.

'I'm the woman who had sex up against a wall, and felt
nothing, presumably? I'm a robot—an automaton.' Her voice
was rising. 'I'm a frigid, sexless, boring spinster—'

'Hardly frigid,' he cut in mildly.

She made a sound like an angry bear, which made it all the
harder for him to hide his smile.

Forget all things sexual? That had been her plan. She should
have known Rigo would make this hard for her. His confidence
was obvious in the way his lips tugged in anticipation of victory,
as if nothing she could say would have the slightest effect on his
arrogant assumption that she would sign his wretched contract
without alteration or complaint. How dared he look at her and
smile? How dared he use that look to stir erotic thoughts?

But—and it was a big but—he was offering her the chance
to do something exciting and different. Living in Italy was
that, even if she didn't know the precise detail yet. Had she
come all this way in attitude and distance only to wimp out
now? She'd pin him down and then she'd decide. Drawing
herself up, which brought her—well, almost to his shoulder,
she suggested, 'Can we sit down and talk?'

Could they? He kept his expression carefully neutral.

A negotiation beckoned. Now that he'd woken the tiger
inside Katie Bannister, there was no way he wanted to see her
vulnerable again. This was his type of woman. The type of
woman he would like working alongside him, he amended.
Katie Bannister had passed the interview process with flying
colours and was definitely the type of feisty, focused individual his foundation needed on the board.

She was sitting at the desk, waiting for him. He leaned his hip against it and looked down. She looked too, but not into his eyes. Not that he was any measure of propriety and chaste thought. 'I'm going to tell you everything,' he said, reclaiming her attention. 'The club I run—'

'The club?' she interrupted, snapping into attack mode. 'I would never leave England for Italy to work in a club, Rigo. I'm sorry,' she said, standing up, 'but I really don't think there's any point in continuing this conversation—'

He cut her off at the door, one fist pressed against it. 'Now you listen to me.' His gaze dropped to her lips.

'And if I won't?'

He might kiss her?

Mild eyes flashed fire. 'Let me go, Rigo…' She rattled the door handle.

'Not until you tell me what you're hiding.'

'What I'm hiding?'

But her eyes told him clearly that she was. 'I know you're hiding something; you're not leaving here until I know what it is.'

'I'm your prisoner?'

He allowed himself a smile. 'If you like.'

Her jaw worked and then she said, 'All right—but not here, not now. Please, Rigo, let's sort out one thing at a time.'

He ground his jaw as she stared unflinchingly into his eyes. Questions competed in his mind. Why the pretence? Why had she pulled back, not once, but twice when they were so heavily into pleasure? Katie had no difficulty enjoying sex. It was anything deeper she shied away from. So what was Katie Bannister hiding from? Him? Men in general? Everyone? He had to remind himself how much she would benefit his foundation if he kept this rigidly confined to business. 'Please sit down again,' he said.

She still looked unsure. He could hear her thinking, work in a club? 'Before you jump ship you should make sure you're not jumping to conclusions. I'm going to tell you about my club and I'm asking you to hear me out. I think you'll be glad if you do—'

'So you trust me now?'

'As much as you trust me. Shall we?' He angled his chin towards the chair at the opposite side of the desk. He didn't turn to see if she was following; something told him she would be. Katie couldn't resist a challenge any more than he could and her curiosity was fully roused.

She walked towards him with her head held high until there was just the desk between them. Resting her fingertips on the edge, she remained standing. Leaning forward to make her point, she said, 'When I was a girl saving up to go to music college I checked coats and served drinks and I considered myself lucky to have a job in a club, but that was then and, at the risk of sounding ungrateful, I don't want to—'

'Pole dance?' he suggested dryly. 'Why don't you sit down, listen to what I have to say first and then give me the lecture?'

'On one condition—'

'Name it.'

'You take me seriously?'

'Believe me, I do take you seriously.' He would like to take her very seriously indeed and the only reason he hadn't taken the relationship to the next level was that Katie was holding him off.

Pulling out the chair, she sat down. 'I promise to hear you out.'

He ignored the rush of interest in his groin and concentrated on the scrapbook in front of him. He spun it round so it was facing her. 'This is my club…'

She went very still as she turned the pages and then she looked at him.

He shrugged. What could he say? This was his life's work, and had been the only thing he cared about and worked for…up to now. The fact that he had never forgotten his roots, or that by assisting these children he was not only helping them but also somehow healing the child he had once been, was his concern, and his alone. The fact that he was sharing this with Katie was a measure of his respect for her. She must stay, and not because revealing this had bared his soul. He knew his secret would be safe with her, but he wanted her to stay because he couldn't imagine life without her. She was a remarkable woman, this self-effacing, quiet, kind girl, and he knew he would never meet anyone like her again.

Katie studied the image on the first page. Rigo was standing in the middle of a small group of men dressed in motor-racing red. They all looked tanned and fit and wealthy, and they all had their arms casually draped across each other's shoulders. At that point she was still thinking the worst of him, but then she moved on to the second page and everything inside her went still. As misjudgements went, hers had been enormous. 'I don't understand…'

'What's to understand?' he said, frowning. 'How can you look at those photographs and tell me you don't want to become involved?'

Rigo's organisation fulfilled as many of the dreams of sick and disadvantaged children as it could. 'So that's why you were racing round the track when I arrived?' Each of the photographs was dated, and as she traced the image for that day lightly with her fingertips her heart filled with admiration and love for him. 'And your friend—the one who was in hospital having the life-saving operation…'

Rigo didn't answer and his expression didn't flicker. He took no credit for any of this, she realised, and even now he wouldn't reveal the identities of any of the families he helped. Now she understood that it wasn't his privacy he guarded so assiduously, but that of the children and their families and his friends.

'The children do occasionally make me late for appointments,' he admitted, smiling faintly.

One glance into Rigo's eyes told a world of stories and, while some of them were happy, many were sad.

'As far as I'm concerned,' he said, 'the children come first. Well, Katie? Now I've explained why I need someone to help me with the expansion of the scheme, how do you feel?'

Rigo would stop at nothing to continue this work. Even his much vaunted pride counted for nothing in Rigo's mind compared to these children. How did that make her feel? Her heart was aching with love for him. She wanted the job. It was a job she could devote her life to willingly and without question. She could feel passion for the job, a passion that would never falter, but—

'I should warn you,' Rigo said, interrupting Katie's thoughts with a condemning glance at her dull brown suit, 'that everyone involved in the scheme is under orders to inject fun and colour into the lives of those we help—'

'And must embrace a more extensive palette than brown, I take it?' she suggested in the same dry tone.

A half-smile creased his face in the attractive way she loved. 'As you can see from the scrapbook,' he said, looking at it, 'you must wear whatever is appropriate for the activity you're taking part in.'

'I draw the line at a yellow jumpsuit.' She was remembering one of the most hair-raising photographs with one part of her brain, and longing for something that could never be with the other part.

'If you do a tandem parachute jump with me, Katie, the yellow jumpsuit is required equipment.'

Bizarrely, as he spoke a wedding dress flashed into her mind. She smiled it away, thinking of the children and the wonderful opportunity Rigo had put in front of her.

'We have to do anything that's asked of us.'

'I understand,' she said.

'Are you ready to give me your answer?' he said. 'Will you join us?'

CHAPTER EIGHTEEN

SHE would do anything for him right now.

Don't give up, Katie's inner voice begged, while common sense told her she could have the job of her dreams, but not the man. Maybe Rigo was playing with her in the sexual sense, Katie reasoned, but she knew he was wholly sincere about his scheme. Perhaps she should choose the security of home over the freedom and romance she had always longed for—at least if she did that her heart wouldn't ache constantly.

She smiled. She knew. There'd never been any doubt what she would do. 'I'll go and put on my new suit, shall I?'

Rigo relaxed. He understood the code. He had offered her the chance to make the difference she had longed to make and she was saying yes.

And now they were both on their feet.

'I can't tell you how pleased I am!' Rigo exclaimed as he came around the desk. 'Thank you so much for agreeing to join us, Katie. I'm going to turn Carlo's legacy into something wonderful. I've already decided I'll keep a small apartment here, but the Palazzo Farnese is going to become Carlo's Kids' Club—'

'So your stepbrother will be remembered for all the right reasons…'

'He will.'

'It's a great name—fun and friendly.' Could hearts explode? Katie wondered as hers pounded violently in her chest.

'I'm already talking to my team of doctors to make sure the centre is everything it needs to be and I'll build their suggestions into my plans—'

'I'll do anything you ask,' she interrupted. 'I mean it, Rigo. I want to be part of this.'

'Welcome to the team, Katie.'

He grasped her hand and let it go. 'This is a big ask.' He stared directly into her eyes. 'I need more than a personal assistant.'

She didn't breathe.

'I need someone like you to speak independently on the steering committee.'

She pulled herself together. 'Of course.'

This was so much more than she had hoped for, Katie told herself firmly. 'I only wish I'd understood all this from the start.'

'Would it have made a difference?'

Rigo's eyes searched hers relentlessly and they both knew he wasn't talking about business now. She knew she looked uncomfortable, but it couldn't be helped. She'd lost the art of masking her feelings the day Rigo had kissed her.

She was thankful when he let it go.

'People's lives are precious,' he said, referring to his scheme, 'and they are entitled to discretion from us.'

'You have my word,' she said, knowing Rigo's foundation was infinitely more important than her own small world of doubt and negative self-image issues.

'The last thing the families need is the media spotlight focused on them—and my friends aren't too happy about it either,' he confessed with a wry smile. 'It's better for everyone if we keep it low-profile.'

'Everything you have told me will remain between you and

me,' she promised him. 'The details of your foundation are safe with me.'

'I never doubted it.'

But there was a question in his eyes. And that question was: why couldn't she be as open with him?

And then with an effortless switch of tempo, he became her boss again. 'I can't wait to get started. I'm so glad you're joining us, Katie.'

In his enthusiasm he caught hold of her arms and spun her round. They were both on a high. And Rigo was an impulsive man. Still, the last thing she had expected was that he would kiss her on the mouth…

The kiss was like no other they'd shared. The impulse and joy that caused it changed instantly to something more. Once reignited that fire raged unabated. She couldn't press herself close enough or hard enough. She had to taste him and feel him in every part of her. She could barely drag in enough air to sustain life…

Rigo swung her into his arms and strode out of the room. He didn't walk up the stairs, he ran.

Closing her eyes, she nuzzled her face into his chest. She was hiding from reality and intended doing so until the last bubble burst. Having mounted the stairs, he shouldered his way into his apartment. It was as shabby as her own, but to Katie's eyes it was equally charming and comfortable. Thanks to the attentions of a reinvigorated staff, it was also spotlessly clean, and as Rigo launched them both onto the super-sized bed she inhaled the faint scent of sunshine and lavender contained in crisp white bedlinen.

'Are you happy?' he demanded, drawing her into his arms.

She could never express how she felt. There was such joy in the air, such exuberance and laughter, and for every nanosecond left to her she was going to live this out to the full.

While he was kissing her Rigo removed her jacket and tossed it away. 'Remind me to make a bonfire for that old suit,' he said, raising his head to look into her eyes, and while she was laughing her skirt followed the same trajectory. All that remained now between Rigo and her scars were her under-wear and a blouse. The last bubble was about to be burst. She turned her face away. It was wrong to allow this. She would not cause him any more pain.

He searched for her lips with his.

She pushed him away. His eyes flickered and changed. She'd hurt him. There was no way not to hurt him. It broke her heart to do this, but it would destroy them both if she let him see her scars. Rigo would turn away from her in disgust, believing he'd been betrayed again.

But she should have known he wouldn't be so easily dis-suaded. She let him kiss her one last time and felt her heart soar. When he released her she stared at him to imprint every atom of his features on her mind. Reaching up, she wove her fingers into his thick black hair, loving the way it sprang, glossy and strong, beneath her palm. She needed that sensa-tion branded on her mind to sustain her in a future without him. In Katie's world love was a cause for concern. Whatever she felt for Rigo must be rigorously controlled so it never reached past the bedroom door.

Yes, and look where she was now…

Touching his fingers to her chin, Rigo made her look at him. 'What are you frightened of, Katie?'

Instead of answering, she traced the line of his beloved face with her fingertips until he captured her hands and kissed each fingertip in turn. Her skin was still prickling from contact with Rigo's sharp black stubble. Tears welled in her eyes as the thought, sharp and dark, like the end of this romance, rose in her mind; there could be no happy ending.

'So, *signorina*,' he murmured against her lips, 'have you no answer for me? Will you not tell me what is wrong, so I can help you?'

What is wrong? I love you with all my heart, she thought, and always will. My love for you fills every part of me with happiness... But she would never speak of this to Rigo. He was so confident and so happy. He was still at the top of the mountain, while she was rapidly slithering down it—though his sexy, slumberous eyes had begun to gain an edge of suspicion. In that brief moment she saw the same vulnerability everyone felt when they had bared their soul to another. And right on cue her scars stung a reminder of why this love for Rigo must go no further.

She pulled away. He dragged her close, kissing her until her soul was as bare as his. He tasted her tears and pulled back. 'What aren't you telling me? Is there someone else?'

'No!' she exclaimed; the idea was abhorrent to her. But Rigo's voice had turned cold and everything had changed. Their brief idyll was over.

'Katie?'

Someone else? No. Something else.

'I knew it.' He thrust her away. 'I can see it in your eyes.'

Could he? Could he see the ridged skin—the ugly, ruined skin? Those foul red shiny scars stood between them as surely as another person—

'Why don't you just admit it?' He launched himself from the bed.

Because she had wanted this too much.

But she had forgotten Rigo was not the tame, civilised man he appeared to the wider world, but a man who had survived life on the streets, fighting for every piece of bread he put in his mouth. Rigo had never stopped fighting, whether for his foundation or for his company and employees, or anyone else he believed needed someone to champion them, and he wasn't about to lose this fight. Whirling round, he seized her wrists and tumbled her back onto the pillows. Holding her firmly in place, he cursed viciously in her face. 'Not again! Do you understand me, Katie? Tell me the truth. Tell me why you have such a problem with commitment.'

'There's no one else—'

'And I should believe you?'

But his grip had loosened fractionally.

'I swear, Rigo—there's only you.'

He let her go and sank down on the bed with his head in his hands.

'You're my world,' she said. 'You fill my mind every waking moment and my dreams are full of you when I'm asleep—'

'Then I don't understand,' he said, looking up. 'What's standing between us? Tell me, Katie. I have to know. Maybe I can help you.'

This big, strong, powerful man, this man who was so confident he could make everything right for her if she only wanted it badly enough. But her voice would never come back and her scars would never go away. Could she burden him with that? Shaking her head, she clung to the edges of her blouse.

Rigo's gaze followed her movement. 'Oh, Katie,' he murmured and, gently disentangling her hands, he brought them to his lips. Letting her go at last, he stood in front of her, stripping off his clothes. When he was completely naked he lay on the bed and drew her into his arms. 'Why couldn't you tell me the truth? Do you think my feelings for you are so fragile?'

As understanding flooded her brain shame suffused her. 'It's not my breasts.'

'What, then?' He went still.

Moments passed and then Rigo drew her to him. 'You have to tell me, Katie. You can't live like this.'

He was right. Without him she was only half-alive.

'I'm going to take your blouse off.' He started unfastening it. He shared his courage, staring into her eyes. He lifted her up into a place he inhabited, a place where problems were dealt with and not pushed aside. He slid the blouse from her shoulders and embraced her back. His hands explored and his expression never wavered. 'Come to me, *cara*,' he said, drawing her closer. 'Trust me…'

And so at last she lay with her face pressed into the pillows while he looked at her back. Hot shame coursed through her. She felt dirty and ugly. She was repulsive. That was how she'd felt when she'd left the hospital and taken a long, hard look at herself in the mirror. Squeezing her eyes shut now, she pictured Rigo recoiling in horror. How could he not? He only had to measure his perfection against her flaws to know jokes didn't come this bad.

But she waited in vain for his exclamation of disgust, and felt the bed yield as he lay down at her side. And then, incredibly, she felt him kiss her back…all down the length of the scars. And when he'd finished, he said softly, 'Tell me—how do you think this changes you?'

'Isn't it obvious?' she mumbled, her voice muffled by the pillows.

'Not to me. Is this what you were hiding from me?'

She turned her head to look at him.

'I can't believe it,' Rigo murmured. 'I can't believe you would think me so shallow—'

'I don't. I think you're perfect—so perfect, how can you not be disgusted?'

'By you holding out on me, perhaps that might disgust me, but by these? You said you'd trained as an opera singer when we were at Gino's, and the letter of introduction sent to me by your firm mentioned it, but it said nothing about a fire—'

SUSAN STEPHENS

'I didn't put it on my CV. I didn't think it relevant to my new life.'

'So you shut it out and tried to forget you were in a fire that left you badly scarred and stole your voice away? And every day you were reminded of what you'd lost each time you spoke or when you took your clothes off.'

'It's not so bad—'

'Not so bad? You lost the future you'd planned. That's big—huge, Katie. Who did you confide in? No one!' he exclaimed when she remained silent. 'And you've been hiding your feelings ever since?'

'I had to hide my scars from you—'

'Because you thought I would throw up my hands in alarm?'

'Because I thought they would sicken you. I thought if you saw them they would take any feelings you might have for me and turn them sour and ugly.'

'So how do you feel now when I tell you that I love you?'

'You—'

'Sì, ti amo, Katie. I will always love you. I can't imagine life without you. You're my life now.'

He stopped her saying anything with a kiss so deep and tender, she felt cherished and knew the nightmare that had mastered her for so long didn't exist in Rigo's mind. Bottling things up, just as he had said, had allowed the consequences of the fire to ferment and expand in her imagination until they ruled her life. And now he was kissing her in a way that sealed the lid on those insecurities. There was no need for words; this was the ultimate reassurance.

Rigo made love to her all night and they woke in the morning with their limbs entwined, when he made love to her again while she was still half-asleep. To wake and be loved was the miracle she had always dreamed of, only it was so much better in reality. 'I love you, Rigo.' She said this, kneeling in front of him, naked. 'You've made me strong.'

'You've always been strong,' Rigo argued. Taking hold of her hands, he drew her to him. 'You just needed reminding how strong you are. If you weren't strong you wouldn't have chosen such a challenging path through life—first music, and now me.'

She laughed. How could she not? 'I love you so much,' she whispered, staring into his eyes.

'You're sure?'

'You made it possible for me to love.'

'So now the world is your oyster?' he teased in his sexy drawl.

'My world is you—'

'*Brava,*' he murmured with one of his killer smiles. Lowering her onto the bank of pillows beside him, he added, 'Just remember, I love every part of you—not just this leg, or that finger, or these ears. I love the whole Katie.'

And the fierce pledge in his eyes said that as far as Rigo was concerned her scars did not exist. 'I love every part of you that goes to make you the woman I love now and always.'

And to prove it he moved down the bed.

As she cried out with pleasure he took her again, and this time when they were one her heart sang.

They had a leisurely breakfast in bed, planning the future. They had already discussed the possibility of Katie seeing a plastic surgeon, should she want to, but for some reason the one thing that had obsessed her since the fire seemed unimportant to her now. Rigo had made it so. He had taken her internal compass and pointed it towards the future—a future they would enjoy together. 'But we will have to leave the room sometime,' she pointed out when Rigo's eyes darkened in a way she recognised.

'But not yet,' he insisted, drawing her down beside him.

'No, not yet,' she agreed.

And when he finally released her, she admitted, 'I fell in love with you the first hair-raising moment we met.'

'I was a brute.'

'You were challenging.'

'And you were very patient with me.'

'And just look at my reward…'

'Ah, there is that.'

Modest to the last, Katie thought, recognising the wicked smile.

'And, Katie—'

'Yes?' she whispered as Rigo drew her beneath him.

'Have you never considered singing again?'

'Now?'

'Later, perhaps,' he suggested, easing into her. 'But just think how the public would love your sexy, breathy voice. If I can fall in love with that voice over the phone—'

'But that's you…'

'Are you daring to suggest there's something wrong with my judgement?'

He was making it very hard to think at all. 'If I did that I would have to question your love for me,' she managed on a shaky breath.

'And you won't, so have some confidence, Katie. There is more than one popular style of music. You can still sing in tune, can't you?'

She was supposed to answer while he was making every part of her sing? 'Well, yes, but I can't sing as I used to—' She gasped as he moved up a gear.

'Your new public wouldn't want you to—'

'My? Oh…' She conceded defeat. No thought possible.

'Have you forgotten that one of my passions is making dreams come true? And I have a keen nose for business.'

She could only groan her agreement.

'You're going to record a track—an album—' he picked up pace '—and who knows? I might even make some money out of you.'

'Rigo, you're impossible,' she shrieked, recognising his game now. Rigo distracted himself while he concentrated on her pleasure.

'I try my very best,' he admitted, still moving as she quietened.

She had no doubt that he would.

CHAPTER NINETEEN

SUMMER came and went in a flurry of love and activity. It was almost Christmas before Katie knew it. The renovations to the *palazzo* were well under way, and she was fully involved in Carlo's Kids' Club. She had started this sunny December day in the kitchen at the Palazzo Farnese, where she was helping to prepare a special lunch for Antonia, who was travelling to see them on one of her regular visits from Rome. Katie was closer than ever to Antonia, having persuaded Rigo that, if she wanted to, his sister must play a full part in his scheme. She had pointed out that Antonia wasn't too young to face up to life and that, if Rigo insisted on shielding his little sister and sent her shopping all the time, Antonia would never grow up. Antonia had embraced this idea with the enthusiasm only Antonia could, and even Rigo had admitted then his sister had been brushed aside for far too long, both by his father and her mother, and then by him. Antonia had seized the opportunity to prove herself and had more than repaid Katie's faith in her, and now they were not just friends but soon to be sisters—

'Hey, *tesoro*.'

Katie's heart bounced with happiness as Rigo walked into the room. She would never lose the sense of excitement she felt each time she saw him.

Walking up to her, he swung her round to face the staff and, leaning his disreputable stubble-shaded chin on the top of the shiny tumble of hair she always wore down now, he announced, 'I have a surprise for you, *tesoro*—'

'Another surprise?' Katie exclaimed.

There had been nothing but surprises from Rigo since the day she moved in—not just to the *palazzo*, or the penthouse, but into Rigo's life. The wardrobe of clothes she had initially refused had miraculously appeared in her dressing room. And when she had asked him where they came from, he said, 'They must have been brought by fairies.' And when she finally stopped laughing, he admitted that he had given most of her measurements to the designers, and that her short audience with them when she first arrived had been a ruse.

'How did you do that?' she demanded.

'I have a good eye,' he admitted.

'Two good eyes,' she remembered telling him with a scolding look. Goodness knew where Rigo gained that sort of experience—and, frankly, she didn't want to know. 'You mentioned a surprise?' she reminded him now.

'Just a little something,' he said, delving into the pocket of his jeans. 'It's something for the wedding. See what you think. I got the colour scheme right, didn't I? White and ivory with a garnish of red roses…?'

Their wedding… She could hardly believe it. Two more days and they would be married at the cathedral in Farnese. 'You know you did,' she rebuked him playfully, wondering what could be in the beautifully wrapped box, with its iridescent ivory wrapping paper and rose-red ribbon.

'Well, open it,' Rigo prompted.

It must be a lacy garter, Katie thought, ripping the paper in her excitement. As the ribbon fluttered to the ground, Rigo caught it and handed it to her. 'Open the box,' he said.

She did so and gasped.

Everyone gasped.

Rigo affected a frown. 'Is blue-white straying too far from your original scheme?'

A huge blue-white diamond solitaire winked at her from its velvet nest.

Katie collected herself. 'Blue-white,' she said, lips pressing down as she pretended to think about it. 'I think it will tone quite nicely.' She turned to him, a smile blooming on her face.

'Is it big enough?' Rigo demanded.

Did Rigo ever do small? 'It's absolutely perfect,' she breathed, 'but you really didn't have to—'

'But I wanted to.'

'Then that's different.'

'Let me put it on your finger.'

He stared deep into her eyes as he did so, and all the staff gave them a round of applause.

'So you finally did it!'

Everyone turned as Antonia bounded into the room. A haze of vanilla and raspberry perfume accompanied her. Antonia's first hug was for Katie. 'My new sister!' she exclaimed. 'At least, you will be in two days' time.' She turned to Rigo. 'You took long enough,' she accused him. 'I thought you would never get round to asking Katie to marry you.'

'A week is too long?' He exchanged a glance with Katie.

'In my world it's forever!' Antonia exclaimed with a sigh. 'And now it's almost four months later, so you have no excuse—there's only me to sort out now—'

'Some day your prince will come,' Rigo interrupted, handing Antonia another box.

'I thought you didn't like shopping?' she accused him, staring at the gorgeous box with wide, excited eyes.

'For my wife-to-be and for my sister, I made an exception to that rule. I bought your gift with Katie along to guide me to thank you for being our chief bridesmaid.'

'There would have been trouble if I hadn't been your chief bridesmaid,' Antonia assured him.

Another amused glance was exchanged between Katie and Rigo. They didn't doubt it.

Antonia's fingers trembled as she held up the slim white-gold chain. 'Rigo, it's *favoloso*!' she exclaimed.

There were two charms hanging from Antonia's chain. The first was a diamond set into a sundial to remind them all to make time for each other, while the second charm was a tiny Cinderella slipper to remind Antonia that her prince would come one day—if she could only be a little patient.

'I love you, Katie!' Antonia exclaimed, throwing her arms around Katie's neck. 'And I have something for you.'

'For me?'

'I have bought you your own journal,' Antonia explained. 'Would you like to see what I wrote in mine that first day we met?'

'Only if you want to show it to me,' Katie said as Antonia delved into her industrial-sized bag.

Antonia extracted the small aqua leather-bound book with a flourish and opened it at the appropriate page. '"I want Katie to marry my brother,"' she announced. 'Well? Am I good at predictions or not?' she demanded, staring at Rigo.

'You're the best,' he admitted, 'and for once we were in absolute harmony, though I fell in love with Katie when I heard her voice on the phone before she even came to Italy. I heard the inner beauty when she spoke, and when I met her I fell in love with her all over again.'

Everyone sighed and it took a moment for life to take

on its regular beat. When it did, Rigo turned to Katie. 'I have another surprise for you, *cara*, which will be revealed over lunch.'

Music was playing as they walked into the sun-drenched orangerie and it took Katie a good few moments to recognise her own husky voice. It sounded quite different when she was singing sultry love songs rather than opera.

'Your first album,' Rigo said, embracing her. 'I hope you like it…'

'As long as you love me, I don't need anything more.'

'Can I have your ring?' Antonia piped up.

'Find your own prince,' Rigo told her as they all laughed.

'I love you,' Katie whispered, staring into the eyes of the man without whom her life might have remained unrelieved brown.

'And I love you,' Rigo murmured, with a darkening look they both recognised, 'for…'

'For?' Katie prompted softly, her gaze slipping to his mouth.

'For allowing me to make a bonfire of that suit—'

'Yay!' Antonia exclaimed, discreetly leaving them to it. 'I love a happy ending…'

EPILOGUE

THE cathedral in Farnese was lit entirely by candlelight. The soft glow brought out the colours of the stained-glass windows and created jewel-coloured garlands on the white marble floor. The scent of the red roses Rigo had insisted on was everywhere, and the angelic voices of a children's choir provided the only fitting soundtrack for a bride and groom who had dedicated their lives not only to each other, but also to their children's foundation. Each ancient wooden pew was decorated with roses secured by a cascade of cream lace, which echoed the glorious floral arrangements throughout the cathedral supervised by the housekeeper and staff of the newly opened children's centre at the Palazzo Farnese. Guests had come from all over the world to celebrate this wedding, but the place of honour was given to Katie's friends from the office and to Gino and his wife from the pizzeria in Rome, while the young maid who had first lent Katie a swimming costume was now a bridesmaid.

Everyone applauded as the Principe and Principessa Farnese walked down the aisle. Rigo had never looked sexier in the dark, full dress uniform of a prince of the line, with a wide crimson sash across his powerful chest, while his bride wore a cream velvet cloak lined with ivory silk satin and, beneath that, a fitted guipure lace dress, frosted with diamonds. There were more diamonds in Katie's hair and on the diaphanous veil that billowed behind her. In fact, there was only one anomaly in Katie's modest outfit—her crimson shoes. 'It doesn't do to be too predictable,' she warned Rigo, smiling when he spotted them.

'I love your shoes,' he murmured, bringing Katie into the sunlight so the crowd could see their new princess. 'Life could be so bland and boring without any surprises—though something tells me life will never be that with you around, Signorina Prim.'

As he spoke the cathedral organ swelled with uplifting chords and mellow tonal resolutions in celebration of a true love story between Prince Arrigo Ruggiero Farnese and Katie Bannister, and as the crowd cheered them to their horse-drawn carriage Rigo squeezed Katie's hand and asked her, 'Happy?'

'How could I not be happy?'

His face creased in his attractive curving smile as he helped her into the golden carriage. 'I guess you must like the fact that we Italians laugh, cry and make love on a grand scale.'

Amen to that, Katie thought as she embraced her new world.

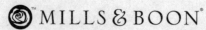

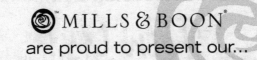

millsandboon.co.uk Community

Join Us!

The Community is the perfect place to meet and chat to kindred spirits who love books and reading as much as you do, but it's also the place to:

- ■ **Get the inside scoop from authors about their latest books**
- ■ **Learn how to write a romance book with advice from our editors**
- ■ **Help us to continue publishing the best in women's fiction**
- ■ **Share your thoughts on the books we publish**
- ■ **Befriend other users**

Forums: Interact with each other as well as authors, editors and a whole host of other users worldwide.

Blogs: Every registered community member has their own blog to tell the world what they're up to and what's on their mind.

Book Challenge: We're aiming to read 5,000 books and have joined forces with The Reading Agency in our inaugural Book Challenge.

Profile Page: Showcase yourself and keep a record of your recent community activity.

Social Networking: We've added buttons at the end of every post to share via digg, Facebook, Google, Yahoo, technorati and de.licio.us.

www.millsandboon.co.uk

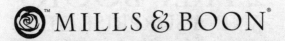

2 FREE BOOKS
AND A SURPRISE GIFT

We would like to take this opportunity to thank you for reading this Mills & Boon® book by offering you the chance to take TWO more specially selected books from the Modern™ series absolutely FREE! We're also making this offer to introduce you to the benefits of the Mills & Boon® Book Club™—

- **FREE home delivery**
- **FREE gifts and competitions**
- **FREE monthly Newsletter**
- **Exclusive Mills & Boon Book Club offers**
- **Books available before they're in the shops**

Accepting these FREE books and gift places you under no obligation to buy, you may cancel at any time, even after receiving your free books. Simply complete your details below and return the entire page to the address below. You don't even need a stamp!

YES Please send me 2 free Modern books and a surprise gift. I understand that unless you hear from me, I will receive 4 superb new books every month for just £3.19 each, postage and packing free. I am under no obligation to purchase any books and may cancel my subscription at any time. The free books and gift will be mine to keep in any case.

Ms/Mrs/Miss/Mr_____ Initials _____

Surname _____

Address _____

_____

_____ Postcode _____

Send this whole page to: Mills & Boon Book Club, Free Book Offer, FREEPOST NAT 10298, Richmond, TW9 1BR

Offer valid in UK only and is not available to current Mills & Boon Book Club subscribers to this series. Overseas and Eire please write for details.. We reserve the right to refuse an application and applicants must be aged 18 years or over. Only one application per household. Terms and prices subject to change without notice. Offer expires 31st December 2009. As a result of this application, you may receive offers from Harlequin Mills & Boon and other carefully selected companies. If you would prefer not to share in this opportunity please write to The Data Manager, PO Box 676, Richmond, TW9 1WU.

Mills & Boon® is a registered trademark owned by Harlequin Mills & Boon Limited. Modern™ is being used as a trademark. The Mills & Boon® Book Club™ is being used as a trademark.